Checked Out

at the

SNOWY
PLOVER INN

Deanna Nese

Books in the Snowy Plover Inn series

Christmas at the Snowy Plover Inn (a novella)
Checked Out at the Snowy Plover Inn

Checked Out

at the
SNOWY
PLOVER INN

Snowy Plover Inn Cozy Mysteries, Book 1

Deanna Nese

Secret Staircase Books

Checked Out at the Snowy Plover Inn
Published by Secret Staircase Books, an imprint of
Columbine Publishing Group, LLC
PO Box 416, Angel Fire, NM 87710

Book layout and design by Secret Staircase Books
First e-book edition: May, 2025
First paperback edition: May, 2025

* * *

Publisher's Cataloging-in-Publication Data

Nese, Deanna.
Checked Out at the Snowy Plover Inn / by Deanna Nese.
p. cm.
ISBN 978-1649142160 (paperback)
ISBN 978-1649142177 (e-book)

1. Snowy Plover Inn (Fictitious locale). 2. California coast—
Fiction. 3. Amateur sleuths—Fiction. 4. Women sleuths—Fiction. I.
Title

Snowy Plover Inn Cozy Mystery Series : Book 1.
Nese, Deanna., Snowy Plover Inn cozy mysteries.

BISAC : FICTION / Mystery & Detective.

813/.54

For my family, especially Mom, who requested a mystery

Acknowledgements

Oh, California, I thank you for your ever-inspiring coastline that always calls me home.

Thank you to my trusted critique partners for your support and suggestions: Phyllisann Maguire, Shirley O'Neil Robertson, Melinda Belcher, and Amy Iori. Thank you to my beta readers for your thoughtful reading and attention to detail: Paula Webb, Marcia Koopmann, Susan Gross, Eve Osborne, Dawn Hasiotis, Isobel Tamney and Gabi Hoffknecht. Many thanks to Stephanie Dewey and Lee Ellison at Secret Staircase Publishing for helping me bring this story to the world.

Chapter 1

Sunday
Maxine

Maxine could scarcely keep her nervous anticipation in check. Pacing, she squelched the urge to check the time, again. She trusted Pearla would set up the lounge and make it all perfect for her first official guests at the Snowy Plover Inn. At six forty-eight a.m., Pearla's text came and Maxine scrolled through the photos taken only moments before. Of course, Pearla had thought of sending photos. *She knows me so well.*

The images depicted sweet rolls and fresh fruits beautifully arranged on the long distressed wooden table along with peeled hard-boiled eggs and artisan cheese wedges. The last text was a video. Max touched it and grinned as Pearla spoke, turning the camera on herself, then aiming it around the living room.

"I've got this, Max. Coffee's plugged in; everything's ready. I'll just fade into the background, tidy up the kitchen, and stay close if anyone needs anything. Stop worrying." *Easy for you to say.* Still, hearing Pearla's confident voice helped soothe Max's nerves.

No guests had stayed at the inn for the last three weeks. Max had taken the time to get settled and assess what she'd gotten herself into. And now, her official first week, only five of the eleven rooms were occupied, left over reservations from before she'd purchased the inn. Three rooms on the second floor of the original structure consisted of the large king suite, and two small singles that shared a bathroom at the end of the hall. The other eight rooms had been added years later extending off the back of the house with four on each side and the courtyard nestled in the middle. The upper rooms were accessed by an exterior staircase and the lower ones each opened onto the courtyard.

The previous owners, a husband-wife team, had assured her there were always regulars, and she'd never need to worry about making the mortgage payments. The inn was a beloved fixture of Silvermist Point even if it had fallen into disrepair of late. *Then why sell it? Why not spruce it up yourselves?* Max questioned, riddled with self-doubt and second thoughts.

She had bought it on a whim. She'd come alone for a weekend getaway, hoping to recapture the magic she'd felt here as a girl with her best friend, Charlene, and Char's devoted parents. Max noticed the For Sale sign, small and discreet, tucked into the overgrown bushes by the main entrance, almost as if it didn't want to be seen, or only wanted the right person to notice it. *It wouldn't hurt to inquire.*

"Is it for sale?" There was a timidity in her voice as she asked the couple who ran it. They were the same owners from thirty-eight years before. *I suppose I can understand why they'd want to retire.* The pair hesitated, as Max witnessed an unspoken communication passing between them. A telepathy born from a lifetime of loving each other and working closely together.

"Are you interested?"

I am.

"I believe I am," she'd responded. "I came here for years with the Thomas Family. I was a friend of their daughter, Charlene. Still am. I haven't been back since high school though. It's been way too long." She thought for a minute. "Thirty-eight years, actually. And I remember why I loved it so much." She was surprised at the sting of tears.

The owners remembered her fondly and had negotiated a more than fair price.

"We want you to have it. We only ask that you don't change it too much." They were disappointed yet understanding that none of their family members had stepped up to take it over. Maxine Egan seemed to be the next best option. At least she knew and loved it. And once they heard her story, how she had lost her husband unexpectedly a year prior, and how she decided to make a big life change to help deal with and distract herself from her grief, they keenly felt she should be the one to take it over. It was a sign from God.

Shortly after seven, Maxine was struggling to resist the urge to walk up the gravel path and see the breakfast service for herself, to feel the space. Then she remembered the video camera discreetly mounted under the wall sconce which would provide her a fisheye view of most of the living room. If only she could figure out how to access it. *How hard could it be?* She opened her laptop, grabbed her glasses, and tried to recall how to access the camera views in real time.

The kid who'd set it up had patiently walked her through and explained how to locate and view the various angles—but she'd been distracted, absently nodding while saying, "Yes, yes, that makes sense." It made little sense though. Nothing technological ever did. And now she was mentally beating herself up for not taking notes. *How long must I wait before heading into the lounge?* If she left now, would the guests think she was lurking? Overly nosey? A busy body? Maxine willed herself to sit and wait. Where was Butters when she needed him? "Here, kitty kitty," she called while shaking the tube of his favorite treats. The buzzing of her cell phone was a welcome interruption. She found it on the kitchen counter, next to her mug of now cold coffee, the foamed milk forming an unappetizing white crust on the edge. It was Char.

"Hey, Char," Maxine said, attempting a lighthearted tone.

"I knew you'd be up. You're dying to go into the living room, aren't you?"

Max glanced around the room before asking her friend, "What? Are you spying on me?"

"Ha! No, but I knew it. Relax! Everything will be fine. Better than fine. Perfect. What time did you get back last night?" Max felt the blush creep up from her neck to her face. *Darned Irish skin. Glad nobody's here to see it.*

"Um, let's just say, late. I lost track of time and didn't want to seem rude to the locals. These people are my neighbors now."

"Right," Charlene replied. "Interesting group, are they?"

"Very," Maxine said as she recalled the evening at Barnaby's. She'd meant to just stop by for a quick burger, fries, and beer, but ended up meeting some locals and joining in for multiple rounds of darts. The folks she met were warm and welcoming and she knew she was destined to spend many more evenings there. It was her kind of place.

"I can't wait to introduce you, especially to Tyne. He's the owner, and trust me, you won't be disappointed," Maxine said with a smile thinking of his ruddy good looks and friendly demeanor.

"I'm intrigued," Char said. "I can hear you smiling."

Before she knew it, it was late. Barnaby's was closing and the first guests had checked in at The Snowy Plover without her there to greet them. Pearla had taken care of everything, sending texts and updates throughout the evening and reassuring Max there was no need to come back, to enjoy herself. At just after 2 a.m. Max had snuggled under the covers with Butters at her side, sleeping only three hours before startling awake.

Charlene always knew the right words to say. She was the calmer of the two friends. Nothing bothered her. Maxine often questioned whether she would have been able to get through this last year without her friend's stalwart presence.

"How's Pearla working out? I bet she's happy to relocate. That was brilliant how you stole her from the school," Char laughed.

"No one stole anyone," Max countered. "Believe me,

she was ready for a change as much as I was. She worked in the cafeteria for twenty-three years, taking crap from the administration and students alike, cleaning up other people's messes. Besides, it was her idea, not mine." It wasn't, if she was being honest.

"Sure, sure. You know I'm kidding. Hey, is anyone booked into our old room? And have you decided if you're going to change it yet?"

Max had, in fact, thought about it a lot, and hadn't decided. There were so many other issues that needed attending to, and that particular room had to be done just right. It could wait.

"No, I haven't done much to the individual rooms yet. A couple is staying in your parents' room and a friend of theirs is staying in ours. Sorry. I wanted you to be able to see the rooms for old time's sake, but Pearla said those rooms were specifically requested. You'll be with me in the cottage though. What is all the background noise, Char? I can hardly hear you."

"I'm driving. Currently on my way to the Snowy Plover Inn. Maybe you've heard of it?"

"Seriously?" Max was relieved and happy. She wasn't expecting Char till the late afternoon.

"Yup. I was going to surprise you, but I should be there in less than forty-five minutes. Hey, I'm almost at the Crossroads exit in Brookhaven. Should I stop? Do you need anything?"

"No, we're all set. I'm only having breakfast and a little wine and cheese reception this afternoon. Pearla's got it all handled. Hey, do you think it's weird if I hang out in the living room?" Max was going to do it regardless. She'd waited long enough, and what was the harm? If she was a guest, she wouldn't think it strange that the owner was there, she would think it was friendly, even charming. Plus, she wanted to foster a vibe of friendliness. Part of her vision for the inn, and herself, was a revolving cast of characters, with repeat players of course, that she could come to know and love. No matter what, she would not be alone or bored. It was just what she needed at this stage in her life. Though her heart would always ache for Adam, her soulmate, she'd already spent the better part of a year in a dark, dark place and she never wanted to go back. She needed to keep living.

"Go ahead. Enjoy it. You are the perfect innkeeper. See you soon."

With Char's blessing, Max hung up and took a quick look in the mirror, still getting used to the shorter haircut falling just above her shoulders. She paused to say to her reflection, "I'm the owner of the inn. I can do this," and she stood a little taller. She grabbed a soft beige angora shawl, slipped on some tall boots, and headed over to the main building. She tried to experience and see the grounds as a guest would.

The air was thick and foggy and moisture dripped from the trees, turning the grass silver. Max followed the path and entered the living room through the French doors off the flagstone patio. There were wrought iron cafe tables positioned just outside the living room, but it was too chilly and damp for guests to sit outside this early, so Max hadn't bothered to properly set them up with linen tablecloths.

Warm air enveloped her as her eyes scanned the room to take in every detail. No guests yet. A golden glow greeted her from the fireplace, it was the only gas one left at the inn, but it used cement logs made to look real. There were restrictions in California on wood burning fireplaces, but the previous owners had replaced them with electric ones that were very realistic and still gave off heat. The odd assortment of chairs and sofas looked cozy and inviting with chunky throw blankets draped over the backs. The inn's furnishings were worn, yet charming. The lending library took up two entire walls and brimmed with the latest reads added from Max's collection alongside some old classics and history books about the area. On either side of the fireplace, the walls were painted a deep hunter green with white built-in shelves.

Several sets of binoculars and bird reference books took up space on a corner bookshelf, and sprinkled throughout were pictures and wooden carvings of Snowy Plovers and other native shorebirds. Over the years, guests had added more to the collection. The newly polished floors gleamed. The furniture would be reupholstered, but kept the same. She had already replaced the area rugs with high quality deep shag in dark blues and dark reds. The living room was a cross between an old hunting lodge, library reading room, and a beachy themed bungalow. Somehow the mash-up worked.

Max had completed no major renovations yet, and she would need to be sensitive and thoughtful when she did. The inn was badly in need of some updating, but the regulars would not appreciate sweeping changes. They came for the familiarity and ambiance. Her challenge would be to keep the regulars returning and to attract newcomers. According to her budget, which she hadn't figured out until after the final purchase papers were signed, Max would need to keep the inn at fifty percent capacity on average through the year to stay afloat and not dip into her meager reserves.

She had funds set aside for renovations, but would need to start small.

Max was delighted, terrified, and thrilled to be her own boss. Admittedly, the endeavor was out of character, but realizing she wanted to plan for her third act in life, whatever that might be, Max took this plunge with an open heart and mind, reasoning that even if it failed, she still would own the property and could sell it, repurpose it, or? As for now, she would enjoy getting to live and work in the place of her dreams.

Disappointed to find herself alone in the living room, Max went through the pantry to the kitchen in search of Pearla. She found her in the front reception area perched on a stool behind the front desk and looking at the newspaper.

"Pearla." The slight woman jumped at the sound of her name.

"Sorry," Max said, joining her. "I didn't mean to scare you. Have you seen any of our guests this morning?"

"I was trying not to lurk." Max heard the excitement in Pearla's voice that matched her own.

"I'm checking every ten minutes and attempting to distract myself with the newspaper. I figure some guests might walk through the lobby on their way to the lounge, so this is the perfect position."

"Good point," Max said as she plopped down on the stool next to Pearla. The two women glanced up to see an older man walk through the lobby. He held his phone to his ear.

"Meet me in the lounge." He paused and glanced around. "She's not up yet. Probably won't be for another hour." His eyes met theirs, and he gave a little wave with his free hand as he continued through to the lounge.

"That's Mr. McMartin," Pearla whispered. "He and his wife checked in yesterday evening. They're staying in room four. Their friend is in room five." She winked at Max, "He's quite the silver fox, huh?"

Max giggled and nodded. "Definitely!"

Minutes later, a woman walked through the lobby.

"Here comes his wife," Max said.

"No, that's Ms. Roxanne Whitam," Pearla said. "She's the friend of the McMartins." Pearla raised her eyebrows. The woman, in a mauve blush velour tracksuit, strode past without looking at them. She sported a high ponytail of frosted blonde hair, and her bright glossy lipstick shined from across the room. At this distance she could be any age.

"Blows me away how some women can look so polished so early in the morning," Pearla sighed.

"True, but you and I both know she didn't roll out of bed like that. That look took at least an hour. No one's ponytail has perfect spirals without a curling iron. And a practiced effort."

"Oh, what the heck. Let's go in," Pearla suggested, while hopping down from her stool.

As Max and Pearla entered the lounge, two additional guests joined them, coming through the patio doors from the courtyard. Max recognized one of them as M. Singer, the author. The other was a man in his forties. Max's nerves calmed, and she felt her confidence level rise. She watched as Ms. Singer poured herself a coffee and sat down in one of the plush recliners. Char had mentioned that she was actually *the* M. Singer, romance writer, and wildly popular with scores of fans buying her books.

Max didn't care for romance novels, but she had heard

of M. Singer. Everyone had. After all, three of her books were on the bestseller list, and when she'd Googled the author, she was further impressed. Apparently, M. Singer had self-published her romance novels and had developed a huge cult-like following. Now all the top publishers wanted to sign her and re-release her previous works. It was every writer's dream.

Max had started writing novels, but hadn't written anything to completion. They sat incomplete and forgotten, what writers refer to as, "drawer babies." Knowing M. Singer was a guest, Max had purchased two used copies of her early titles from Books and Brew in town and placed them on the shelf in the living room. She'd recognized the titles as ones her students often enjoyed. M. Singer had recently released her tenth book and her fans were saying it was the best yet. Max had planned to read at least one before meeting the famous author in person, but she hadn't found the time, and now it was too late. She'd have to fake it. When Ms. Singer made eye contact, Max engaged her in conversation.

"Are you enjoying your stay Ms. Singer?"

"It's so peaceful here, beautiful," she said as she paused and glanced around. "Heavenly!" Max smiled. She had always felt this way about the inn.

"I feel the same. I came here as a girl with my best friend and her family. It's always been a magical place for me."

"Are you the new owner?" Ms. Singer had a pleasant voice, deep and husky, almost masculine. Max thought it would be perfect for audiobooks and wondered if she recorded her own stories, or if she hired someone else to do it.

"Yes, I purchased it a month ago, and I'm officially taking over today, in fact. I'm learning as I go, you could say, but I'm loving it. It'll be an interesting challenge. In my former life, I was a teacher. A wife and mom, too."

"Well, good for you." Ms. Singer seemed genuinely sincere. "I visited the inn once before, and have wanted to return ever since."

"I find it can have that effect," Max agreed. "I plan to update it a bit more, but really, I want to keep the same feeling it's always had. So far, I've polished the wood floors and replaced a few rugs." Not wanting to talk too much, Max ended the conversation with, "Let me know if there's anything you need. And I hope you'll enjoy your stay."

Next Max turned her attention to whom she assumed was Keith Lombard or Parker Graves. Her money was on Keith Lombard. He was a handsome man, and she guessed too mature to be the boyfriend of Char's distant cousin, Krista, age twenty-four, due to arrive sometime today.

"Professor Lombard?" Max asked.

"Yes. Hello. And you are, Max, is it? The new owner?"

"I am. Officially starting today. I thought I'd pop in and say hello to my first guests. I hope you like the breakfast spread."

"I love it, a positive change for sure. I've been staying here for years, and always had to go into town for breakfast. Are these bear claws from The Front Porch Bakery?" He held one up and took a large bite.

"You guessed it," she smiled. "And we'll have a complimentary glass of wine and some cheese and snacks out every afternoon."

The little town was close. Guests of the inn could walk there if they chose, but Maxine's goal was to give them a reason to stay and enjoy the grounds and nearby shoreline. There had always been a little store in the reception area with snacks and local crafts, cold drinks, ice cream bars, and bottles of wine. Max had decided to provide a light breakfast with coffee and pastries from local shops. *Makes it more homey.* This way no one had to get up early in search of a good strong coffee. They could always find it in the living room. So far, so good.

"Professor Lombard," Max began.

"Please, call me Keith," he interrupted.

"Sorry, Keith. Are you still willing to lead an educational 'walk and talk' today about the Snowy Plover? The bird, I mean. Not the inn." He smiled.

"I would be happy to, if any of your guests are interested. Why don't we plan for two o'clock? We can gather here before setting out."

"Yes, perfect. At the very least, it will be me and my friend Charlene who should arrive soon. Possibly her cousin. I'll write it on the chalkboard in the reception area so anyone else who wants to can join us. And thank you. I'm grateful to learn more about the birds."

Next Max approached Mr. McMartin who was sharing a small loveseat with Roxanne Whitam. The two looked very cozy, legs touching from thigh to knee, with Roxanne's arm draped across the backrest and stroking the back of his head. "Hmm," Max thought. "Maybe they're a thruple." It was a term she'd recently learned from her son, Sawyer, and it would explain why they wanted the adjoining rooms. Though why anyone would want to share a man was beyond her, even one as good looking as Mr. McMartin. But wasn't he also like seventy-five? Pearla spoke before she could.

"Is there anything I can get you two, Mr. and Mrs. McMartin, is it?" Max wanted to give her a shove. Pearla knew full well that was not Mrs. McMartin, and she was clearly enjoying stirring the pot. *Why? Must you, Pearla?* Max thought. Roxanne instinctively removed her hand from the back of Mr. McMartin's head as if she just realized what it might look like to onlookers, and answered, "I'm not Mrs. Mc Martin. Just a friend. Right, Walt?" Walt hastened his body to the edge of the small sofa, trying to put some distance between them and looking uncomfortable.

"That's right. We're old friends."

"Who're you calling old, now? You know I'm far younger than you and much younger than Rose," Roxanne teased.

It was fascinating to watch the exchange. Even more so when Rose McMartin appeared as if on cue entering through the reception area. She was subtly attractive, not flashy like her friend Roxanne. She gave her husband a look that no one could miss, disdain with a side of boiled anger, and stood next to Roxanne's half of the sofa. Roxanne made no effort to move. Rose turned her back and grabbed the nearest chair, a large wingback. She dragged it over to face the sofa. Her smooth expression did not fully hide the fury brewing beneath the surface.

"Here Roxanne. I brought you a chair. You can move now." She indicated the chair with a controlled swoop of her hand. "I'm going to get a coffee and some fruit, and I'll be back." She turned her attention to her husband.

"Walt, do you need a refill?"

"No thanks, Dear" he replied sheepishly. As soon as Rose walked away, he hissed, "Move Roxanne, it's not funny. Don't mess with her like that, you know how delicate she can be."

"I'm delicate too," Roxanne pouted. She touched his hand and stood as Rose returned, balancing a plate and a coffee.

"Leaving?" Rose narrowed her eyes and asked pointedly.

"Yes, I think I'll find a book and go to my room. Are we still going into town later?" Roxanne directed her question at Walt, not Rose, but Rose answered.

"No. I want to go down to the shore and hear the presentation from the naturalist. I can't do both. It's too much for me, I think. My knee isn't completely healed yet."

"Oh, I guess I'll come along too," Roxanne said.

The conversation was uncomfortable, yet fascinating to watch, and Max excused herself and Pearla with, "Great, then we'll see you all later. If you need anything, don't hesitate to ask Pearla, or me," and she slowly backed away with Pearla taking the cue to leave as well.

After coffee and some breakfast, the guests were free to explore the grounds, take a swim in the heated pool, relax in their rooms or go into town. Those who wished to join the walk to the shore with Professor Lombard, would meet in the lobby at two.

When the ladies were back in the reception area, and out of earshot, Pearla was first to whisper, "Oh man, that Roxanne is a firecracker. What nerve! I mean the guy's wife is literally right there."

"The walk down to the shore should be interesting watching those two mix it up," Max said as she noticed Charlene's red convertible pull up in front of the inn.

"She's here."

Chapter 2

Charlene

Charlene hung up with her best friend Maxine and cranked up the stereo in her new red Mustang. She alternated her hands on the steering wheel, flexing her fingers to keep the joints supple. Even at fifty, she could turn heads. She was beautiful without trying, but this last flare up was taking its toll. Her rheumatoid arthritis was unpredictable. Sometimes it would go into remission and Charlene would feel as if she had a new lease on life. She would hike and travel and plan activities to exert herself to exhaustion knowing that at any point, the cycle might begin again and leave her virtually disabled and feeling old and depressed. The last flare up settled in her hands and was nearly unbearable. She wasn't able to paint at all and some days even turning the pages of a book would cause her fatigue and frustration. Add to that, the meds often gave her brain fog and made it difficult to focus.

The disease was all but invisible. She looked healthy. Close friends knew she was experiencing a flare up when they saw her face. Her sharp cheekbones and deep dimples were muted and her features rounded by the course of steroids she had to take to get relief. Her strict regimen of yoga and healthy eating kept her in the best place to fight the disease. Travel kept her sane, too.

The Snowy Plover Inn had always been a place of comfort for Max and Char. Charlene was an only child, so by default, her best friend was included in the small family's vacations and other adventures. The inn was a multiple-times-a-year destination, it being an easy three-and-a-half-hour drive from where the girls lived. Every visit, the girls stayed in the same room. Their room was adjacent to Char's parents, had its own bathroom, and was connected with a den in between. Visitors could rent all or part of the multi-room suite. Char's parents were far more lenient and trusting than Max's, and when the girls stayed at the inn, they were allowed to do pretty much anything they wanted.

"Your parents treat us as mature ladies. It's so refreshing," Maxine commented once when they were young teens.

"Huh? Yeah, I guess so," Char said, having never really considered it.

From second through eighth grade, the girls consistently visited the inn three times a year. Four days over winter break, four days over spring break, and one or two weeks over the summer. The inn fit into the regular pattern of their lives and marked the passing of each season as they grew from girls to young women. Their room was always ready, waiting for their return. The girls could picture no one else using the room and thought of it as theirs alone.

In winter during their stay, the twin metal frame beds had thick plaid flannel duvets and there were extra chunky blankets on the sofa and armchairs in the private den. Pinecones and evergreen boughs with red ribbon decorated the coffee table. In springtime, their beds were made up with pastel quilts—a tulip pattern for Char, who always took the bed on the left, and an abstract pattern for Max on the right, though the girls usually pushed the beds together to make a large king sized one where they stayed up whispering and giggling late into the night. For summer, it was bright white matching thin chenille bedspreads with tassels and crisp white cotton sheets.

The scents at the inn were always the same, but changed with the seasons: cinnamon and pine for winter, lavender and vanilla for spring, and coconut and ginger for summer. Once the girls entered high school, the local public school for Maxine and a private academy for Charlene, the visits became sporadic and were no longer a priority.

Charlene jumped out of her car and rushed up the wide front steps, pushing open half of the double door and stepping inside the lobby looking radiant as always with a huge grin. Her unruly curly hair was up in a messy bun and she sported her signature red lipstick. She wore snug black jeans that shouldn't look good, but did on her curvy frame, an oversized white cashmere sweater, and a flowy blue scarf tied perfectly around her neck. Charlene always looked like she consulted daily with a personal stylist and she could pull off any fashion, any mixture of styles and colors. Max had lamented this since they were kids, impressed by best friend but also a tinge jealous of how effortless Char made it look. If Max even tried to pull off some of those combinations, she would look foolish or clownish; this she knew from experience and Char's well-meaning attempts to impart some style tips.

After a long hug and a quick hello to Pearla, Charlene peppered Max with a rush of questions.

"Has Krista arrived? How does she seem? What about her boyfriend? What are the other guests like? Are you at capacity? How did the floors turn out? I can't wait to see the cottage."

"Okay, hold on. No, Krista isn't here yet. Neither is her boyfriend. The guests are charming, you can meet them later during the educational walk with the professor. We're at half capacity so far, floors came out great." She took a breath, "Whew. Now let's go see the cottage, unless you want to grab some coffee and a Danish in the lounge," Max said.

"I can move your car," Pearla offered.

"Yes, please, and we need to catch up too, later."

"Definitely."

Charlene tossed Pearla her keys and followed Maxine into the lounge. Only Ms. Singer remained. Her back was to them and she was looking at the bookshelves. Max silently congratulated herself on thinking ahead to have two of the author's books on display.

"Introduce us," Char whispered. Max responded with wide eyes meant to signal, "No, not now," but Ms. Singer turned to face them and instead Max said, "Ms. Singer, this is my best friend, Charlene. She is staying for the week as well." Char walked over with her hand held out.

"It's nice to meet you. I'm a devoted fan of your books. I've read them all."

"We won't bother you though," Max said.

"Thank you. It's always nice to meet a fan," Ms. Singer replied.

Charlene appreciated the author who wrote her books using a practice called method writing, a process similar to method acting in that the writer fully immerses themself and tries to embody the character to better understand their perspective. Being an erotic romance author, Char wondered what this immersion might look like and was curious to ask M. Singer about it. As well, she longed to ask what the M. stood for. *Maybe later.*

Chapter 3

Rose

Rose and Walter McMartin had stayed at the Snowy Plover Inn before. It was Rose who had suggested this getaway to her husband who lately seemed out of sorts, complaining that his golf game was off. He was irritable and snippy with her and left for hours at a time while leaving his cell phone at home. Rose had tried to search his phone for clues, but was locked out. He'd changed the password and hadn't shared it with her. When she tried to bring up her concerns, he brushed her off, apologized, and acted sweetly for a few days, bringing home flowers or her favorite wine, or even treating her to a massage, which he considered a waste of time.

"I was just at the gym. I don't know what you get so

jumpy about, Rose."

"Am I jumpy?" Rose wondered. After all, Walt was seventy-two and though in great shape, his cholesterol was high and he was a true Type A personality. He'd just passed his fifteenth year of retirement as a firefighter and still looked as handsome as ever. Between coaching the golf team at the local high school, and helping their daughter start a landscaping business, he was constantly busy. Rose had commitments too, but was far more flexible with her time, and if an opportunity to travel came up, she took it.

It was on a cruise that Rose and Walt met Roxanne. She was with her boyfriend; one who she'd long since broken it off with. She and Rose became fast friends. Rose was a natural beauty without trying. She never wore much make-up and dressed well, but comfortably, which was a contrast to Roxanne's need to be noticed. It was a friendship mildly tolerated by Walt. He saw Roxanne as a screechy, never-stops-talking, and an always-about-herself kind of person. Still, he was cordial to the ever-changing array of men Roxanne dated and brought over to their house, but he encouraged the ladies to make their own plans without him. *Until recently.*

Lately Roxanne was involved in everything they did and Rose found it truly tiresome. She'd planned this trip to reconnect with Walt, but Roxanne had seen it on their kitchen calendar and asked, in her own subtle yet pushy manner, to tag along. Rose could think of no kind way to exclude her friend who also was quite dense in taking a hint. She'd even tried to be direct.

"Roxanne, I'd really prefer alone time with Walt. He's been busy and I want us to reconnect. This has always kinda been our go-to place. You understand, right?"

"Yes, but I won't bother you at all. I'm so lonely. I haven't even dated anyone in forever. You're so lucky to have each other. I'll book my own separate room. You won't even know I'm there." Roxanne was adept at getting what she wanted.

Frustrated, but unable to think of a kind way to brush off her friend, Rose had agreed to let her come. And with each passing minute, her regret grew. Her knee was more swollen than usual this morning and the swelling had only slightly decreased even after a thousand milligrams of Motrin, but there was no chance she would back out and leave her husband alone with Roxanne.

Roxanne had joined them for dinner last night, complaining that she didn't want to be by herself and didn't know the area, and then squashed into the booth next to Walt, leaving Rose across from them. *The nerve.* When Rose tried to bring up her annoyance with Roxanne's flirting last night, Walt had brushed her off and even intimated that she was imagining things. *Am I?* He'd encouraged her to double up on her sleeping pill to get a good night's sleep, and after the long drive and late arrival, she'd agreed.

"I wouldn't want you to be tired tomorrow. I know you don't want to miss out on anything," he'd said.

"But why aren't you in your pajamas yet?" Rose asked, noticing he hadn't even removed his shoes.

"Don't worry honey. I might just get some air first," Walt said on his way out the door.

Rose felt her eyelids closing and didn't fight it. She drifted off into a deep sleep, never stirring till morning when she woke to read the note left on his side of the bed that hardly looked slept in. *Going for breakfast. Meet me in the lounge.*

She dressed quickly and smoothed her hair back with a headband, no time for make-up, and headed out. Entering the lounge, her attention was drawn immediately to her husband and supposed friend who were all but snuggled up together on a loveseat.

Chapter 4

Maxine

At five after two, the guests were gathered in the living room. They wore windbreakers and carried packs with water, bird identification books, and snacks. When all were situated, they headed out to the shoreline. Leading the way was Professor Keith Lombard, followed by Max, Char, Walt and Rose McMartin, Roxanne, and Krista. Ms. Singer stayed behind explaining she had a tricky bit of writing to tackle and wanted to "lock in." Parker, Krista's boyfriend, had still not arrived.

"Please call me Keith," the guide requested as they set out from the patio off the living room. The inn had direct access to the trail and if guests went down to the shore on their own, they could call a cell number provided if they needed a ride back. An employee could bring the all-terrain golf cart to pick them up.

"We're going to see a lot of birds this afternoon if we're lucky. I'll show you where the plovers nest and we'll check the netting surrounding the area."

Maxine recalled spotting the little birds during her childhood. She and Char were always very careful not to disturb them during nesting season. Maxine hoped seeing the birds would be special for her guests. It was rewarding to glimpse the babies when they hatched and it was hard not to feel protective toward them. She was glad the inn could play a role in bringing awareness and she pictured hosting field trips for children to come and learn about the birds.

The trail was well maintained; Maxine had seen to that. It was about eight feet wide, covered with wood chips, and it meandered from the back of the property line all the way to the land owned by the conservancy. The inn's property was about ten acres in total and butted up to land owned by the conservancy which could never be developed and extended all the way to the shoreline. It was a relatively flat, easy walk, mostly shaded with a variety of tall pines and other trees and shrubs. One of Maxine's ideas was to market the inn as an eco-destination. The bird conservancy always needed volunteers to help protect the snowy plovers and bring attention to the worthy cause of saving them and increasing their numbers. She listened with her guests as Keith Lombard spoke about the plovers.

"Snowy plovers are threatened because they roost on sandy beaches and sand dunes along the coasts of California, Oregon, and Washington."

"Oh, that's fascinating," chirped Roxanne. "Isn't it,

Walt?" she asked and squeezed his shoulder.

"Why don't you just let him speak, please," Rose said. Maxine could sense the tension.

Oblivious, Keith continued, "Nesting season occurs from early spring to late fall and the females lay their eggs in a shallow scrape of sand leaving them vulnerable to predators, or accidental destruction by off-road vehicles, or even just unaware beachgoers or their off-leash dogs. The eggs take about twenty-eight days to hatch and plovers often return to the same nesting spot yearly."

Besides the plovers, the guests were guaranteed to see sea gulls. Other possibilities at the shoreline included sandpipers, brown pelicans, cormorants, least terns, snowy egrets, and the majestic great blue herons. On the way there, one could often spot red-tailed hawks and sometimes owls.

The Snowy Plover Inn, so named for the diminutive little bird, was ideally located near a remote stretch of coastline infrequently visited by large numbers of people. The coastal area here was an unmanicured windswept beach with lots of driftwood and piles of dried kelp left from high tides. There were high cliffs on either side, so each beach area along this part of the coastline was isolated and only connected when the tide was low. Unsuspecting visitors sometimes found themselves stuck at a beach when the tide rose at mid or high tide. The outcroppings of the cliffs cut each patch of beach off from the next. The inn was positioned in a depression between two high cliff areas. When looking from a bird's-eye view, it might appear like a slice was removed from a pie.

The guests made their way down the path listening and observing as Keith Lombard pointed out the various birds they saw along with the names of certain trees and plants.

Max recalled how she and Char would race down from the inn, in what seemed like minutes, bounding onto the practically private beach, gathering driftwood and making a shelter or adding to one that someone else had built. Occasionally they'd run into others, but more often had the area to themselves. They could write their crushes' names in the wet sand and watch the waves break on the shore, making them disappear. Char's parents trusted them, but not the current, and the girls were forbidden to enter the water past their knees even though both were excellent swimmers.

"If you want to swim," they said, "use the pool. There aren't any lifeguards."

This was fine with Max and Char. The pebble-bottom pool was heated to eighty-three degrees year-round and was designed to look and feel like a natural swimming hole with a sloped entrance and surrounded by native plants. The nearby hot tub was a constant toasty hundred three degrees with a timed dial to turn on the bubbles. So Max and Char enjoyed switching back and forth at all hours of the day and night before settling into their room and cozy beds.

The walk with Professor Lombard was informative and fascinating. Max felt certain the guests were enjoying themselves. Krista was a delight, such a sweet girl and so complimentary towards Char and Max. Shy at first, but she was coming out of her shell.

"I'm so thankful you invited me, Charlene," Krista said. "This place is incredible and I've never really had a vacation of any kind. I just work. A lot."

"Please, you have to call me Char," Char insisted. "After all, we're cousins. And I don't care how many times removed or whatever. I'm just glad to get to know another family member since my parents passed, and I don't have kids of my own. Maxine and her son Sawyer are my closest family. And now you."

Max was pleased that Char had found a family member. Char's father was not her biological father, but that didn't matter. No one could ask for a more devoted dad. He and her mother had always supported anything Char wanted, all her artistic pursuits. Char had never had to trouble herself over money matters, and when he passed, everything was left to her. Millions. Max didn't know all the details, but could easily ask if she was curious. When she called Char to tell her she purchased the inn, Char's first response was, "Let me pay it off for you. Please."

"No," Max had said, ever grateful that her friend had offered with zero hesitation. *This is something I can do myself. I don't want it to feel easy.* Max needed the stakes to be high. She needed a focus, a project, but knowing her friend would never let her fail meant the world to her. This was the first full day with guests and Max percolated with optimism.

As she and the guests returned to the inn, they lucked out by spotting an owl. The bird was camouflaged and blended well with the bark and foliage of the tree. There's no way the guests would have seen him if it wasn't for the professor. Max overheard snippets of conversation between Rose, Roxanne, Walt, and the professor. Roxanne was peppering Professor Lombard with questions while Rose and her husband were holding hands and listening passively. When they were back on the property, Max reminded her guests of the wine and cheese reception. "I sure hope you'll come." Everyone said their thanks and parted ways.

Chapter 5

Rose

Rose stood up placing both hands on the table next to her for balance.

"I'm just going outside to get some air," she said, glancing around the room, but the only person left to hear was Keith Lombard, and he was too wrapped up in whatever he was reading to notice. She walked with confidence toward the patio, the least wobbly she could manage after three glasses of wine and a healing knee and was grateful no one was paying attention to her. She needed another drink. Just a nip, and she couldn't very well indulge in front of Walt, and that insufferable Roxanne. Rose's balance was off, easily explained by the walk down to the shore; it was more strenuous than she remembered, and she'd needed to lean on Walt a little on the way back. She also thought her lack of water intake was a contributing factor, and maybe the muscle relaxer. It was definitely *not* the three glasses of Chardonnay. She could go back to her room and drink a glass of water and take a nap. *I'm not tired though. I'll feel better after one more glass of wine and maybe another snack. Who would notice one bottle?*

Then instead of heading outside, Rose crossed the room and tried the door marked Private. It was the walk-in pantry. A second swinging door led to the kitchen, and when she peeked through, she saw Pearla coming up the stairs from the cellar, pulling the door shut behind her. It too was marked Private. *That's where I'll find the wine.* When Pearla left the kitchen, Rose snuck in and tried the door to the cellar. Of course it wasn't locked. She was sure to find an open bottle here. *If not, I'll open one myself.* Who would notice one bottle? In her coat pocket were a stemless wine glass and bottle opener she'd taken from the lounge. Just one more drink, and she knew she'd feel better. Less tense and judgmental of her friend and her husband. She hoped she was overreacting.

The kitchen would have been too obvious. *Someone might see me.* No one will come to the cellar. Pearla had cleared away the charcuterie board of treats to accompany the complimentary glass of wine the inn provided each guest. When no one was looking, Rose had poured herself a second glass and then a third. Had there been a fourth too? Maybe. The afternoon's events felt slightly less annoying then, but she was still bothered at the obvious flirting between Roxanne and her husband. True, Roxy would often flirt with anything in pants, preferable, and not necessarily male, but this was just too much. This time, even with the presence of another single man, the professor, she had laser-focused all her attention on Walt, and Rose got a sick feeling deep in the pit of her stomach that there might be more to worry about than some harmless flirting.

After the nature walk, Rose requested that she and Walt relax in their room, and he agreed.

"We'll see you later, Roxanne, we're going to our room to rest," Rose said with satisfaction.

"Oh well, I'm not sure what I'll do," Roxanne had replied.

Don't know, don't care, don't care to know. Rose had to bite her tongue not to utter the words aloud.

She and Walt were barely in their room five minutes before the knock came. Walt opened the door and there stood Roxanne in a sheer "cover-up" wearing a bikini she was way too mature for. *Are you frickin' kidding me?*

"Do you guys want to go in the pool with me? Or the hot tub?"

"No, we don't. We'll see you later." But Walt had said yes, not no, and so Rose grabbed her book and curled up on an adjustable chaise by the hot tub while her husband and Roxanne splashed around and acted like teenagers. *Maybe this is the end.* Rose felt demoralized and foolish and wondered how long the affair had been going on right under her nose.

Rose found the cellar door and gently pushed it open. She felt for the light switch and located it on the right. Flipping it on provided weak light on the stairs, but more filtered in below from the tall windows of the basement-like room. There were other goodies stored down here besides wine. Canned jams, spices, artisan olive oils and various seasonal items that were offered for sale in a small display in the lobby. Rose held onto the rail and navigated the narrow steps. Pausing two stairs from the bottom, she caught a chill. The door to the outside was ajar, letting in the cold air. Rose grabbed hold of a metal rack to steady herself and look around. A searing explosive pain in her skull was the last thing she felt.

Chapter 6

Larry Trawl

Larry Trawl, hands on hips, surveyed the scene before him, taking in every detail. An older lady, who he recognized as one of the guests, was lying in a pool of blood. A dented gallon-size metal can of virgin olive oil lay tipped on its side next to her. The plug had sprung loose and the oil mixed with the lady's blood creating a scene that would almost be comical if it wasn't so serious. *Run. Get the hell out of here.* A few minutes passed as he stood frozen, hands in his pockets, before he thought to take her pulse. He felt her wrist. A pulse was faint, but present. Another minute passed before he pulled his phone from his pocket and dialed his son, Colby. The call went straight to voicemail.

"Stupid kid never picks up," he muttered and hung up, shoving his phone into his back pocket. Never mind that the kid was fifty-three. No point in leaving a message. *Had Colby completed the job of stacking the boxes from the delivery?* No, it looked like he had just dropped them in the middle of the room, and hadn't organized them at all. *I'm always having to check his work. Typical.* A corner of one box was touching the blood. He pushed it up to the nearest wall. It was heavy, containing dishware. He grabbed a pile of dish towels from the tall metal shelf and threw them into the bloody puddle. So much blood. He picked up the olive oil can and tried to wipe it off, then he set it to the side.

She was lying in a strange position. He grabbed her legs and straightened her out, pulling her away from the stairs, leaving a trail of broken glass and blood. *Should I sweep it up?* With the side of his shoe, he scooted the larger of the glass shards closer to the woman. He used a bloody finger to check her pulse again, this time gently touching the side of her neck. Noticing her shallow breath, he was relieved that no one could ask why he made no attempt at mouth-to-mouth breathing. How many minutes had he wasted? *What have I done? Will this lady die?* Realizing the gravity of the situation and how his inaction might be perceived, he called his new boss next. She answered on the first ring.

"Ms. Maxine, you need to get down to the cellar right away. There's been an … accident." Mr. Trawl had moved away from the lady. He held the phone to his ear with his shoulder while fully opening the door that led to the exterior of the building. Now he must decide if he should exit, or stay with the body. *Lady, she's a lady, not a body. There simply can't be a dead body at the Snowy Plover Inn. The inn won't recover from this. It must be kept quiet.* These thoughts ran through his mind, and he only half comprehended the voice coming through his phone.

"Mr. Trawl. Mr. Trawl. What happened? Is someone hurt? Who is it, and where are you?"

"The cellar," he replied. "It's the older lady, Mrs. McSomething. There's a lot of blood. But she's not dead. At least not when I checked."

"I'm coming right now. I'll be there in a minute. Is help on the way? Did you call 911?" He hadn't.

"Yes, of course I did. First thing. They'll be here soon."

"Can you tell me what happened?"

"No. I don't think so. Looks like a can hit her in the head. I don't know." He tried to remain calm, but his voice shook.

"Just don't move her. And don't touch anything. We don't know what happened."

"Right."

Mr. Trawl grabbed two more dish towels and wedged them under the woman's head. It looked like that was where the blood was coming from. He picked up the oil can and moved it again, then went up the stairs and opened the door. Now both doors were open and Larry Trawl stood waiting at the top of the stairs. Maxine would be here any second, and he hoped she would enter through the outside door. He remembered then to call 911. With shaky fingers, he punched in the number and waited. The call connected.

"This is 911, what is your emergency?" He blurted out the inn's address to the operator, then said there was an accident.

"It's an older woman with a head injury, that's all I know. Just get here quick."

"Sir, I need you to stay on the line." He heard the directive, but pressed the end call button just as Maxine, his new boss, came in from the outside door. Mr. Trawl wanted nothing more than to leave the scene and let his boss deal with it, so before she could spot him, he slipped out the cellar door into the kitchen and made for the outside as quickly as possible. He needed to find his idiot son and hoped he was far away. He would even be glad for once if Colby was getting wasted at Barnaby's. Just as long as he wasn't anywhere near here. It shouldn't matter though. This was just a clumsy lady who'd taken a spill. Nothing to worry about. No one to blame.

Thankfully, he didn't bump into any guests. *It's not my problem.* He made his way past the pool area, careful to stay behind the shrubbery. No guests were out. He snuck around the pavilion and was relieved that it, too, was empty. On the far edge of the property, he came to the trailer he shared with Colby.

Colby Trawl was one to carry a grudge. If someone wronged him, revenge was his answer. And the revenge would not match the perceived wrong in severity; it often was far worse. This trait had gotten him into trouble frequently in his life. Suspensions, expulsions, community service, and the latest being a five-year prison sentence. He got out in four years and three months for good behavior, and came straight to his father like a prodigal son to beg for a job, any job, and a place to stay.

The elder Trawl caved as always and said Colby could help with maintenance at the inn where he had been employed for his entire adulthood. Larry Trawl knew no other life and planned to stay as long as he could competently do the work. Though keenly aware that his son's hot temper and criminal record might jeopardize his situation, he would not turn him away.

When the previous owners sold the property, they kindly stipulated that Larry Trawl be allowed to keep his position and the new owner agreed to the terms. Of course, it was only an honor-bound verbal agreement and legally there was nothing in the way of Maxine Egan letting him go like an old farm dog whose time has come.

"I wouldn't want to put any of your current employees out of a job," he heard her say. He seized the opportunity to include Colby in that offer of stability, hoping she would not think to do a background check, and that she also wouldn't remember either of them from her childhood visits.

"Oh, yes, my son has worked here with me the whole time. I thought you understood. He would like to keep his job as well." This was something Larry Trawl could do, it was the least, when he felt somehow responsible for the poor life choices Colby made. Colby had cost him his second wife. They separated when Larry refused to put his son out on the street.

"He's a grown man," Beth complained. "You don't owe him a place to live and I will not be in the same house as him." But it was more than that to Larry. He felt a sense of obligation to his only child, so strong he sacrificed his marriage rather than not honor it. He put up no argument when Beth insisted she get to keep the house, though Larry had purchased it many years before. She worked part-time at the fancy grocery store in the village and did not want to leave Silvermist.

Larry made it a point to avoid her. Each time he accidentally ran into Beth, it was too painful. He moved into the second-hand trailer parked on the outskirts of the inn's property. It was tight with two adult men, but he would never ask his son to leave. He only hoped the inconvenient living conditions and lack of privacy would encourage Colby to move out. So far, no luck.

In his darkest, private thoughts, Larry Trawl wondered if Colby was an evil seed and therefore, unredeemable. Other times he saw a troubled and misunderstood child, a victim of cruel classmates. A kid who struggled with academics and friendships and social interactions. When his son's teachers suggested counseling, Larry objected every time, crushed with embarrassment over what it all meant. His kid was odd and different. But he had been too, yet he managed to make a decent life for himself.

Larry had dropped out of high school in ninth grade. He was already sixteen having been held back twice. Like bad history repeating, his son never completed high school either. By junior year, Colby was still technically a freshman as far as credits earned toward a diploma. Like father, like son. There wasn't a way he could graduate with his class. Larry suggested Colby attend night school in order to at least earn a GED. Colby refused. Through the years Colby would disappear and reappear, usually when he was down on his luck or needed money. Larry wanted to know his son was safe, but was also relieved not to have to keep an eye on him.

Colby had his vices too, beginning with his excessive drinking and ending with him using, buying, and selling illegal drugs and ending up in prison. Larry wished he would take the initiative to better his situation, but Colby was content to work the job his father secured for him and live rent-free in the trailer with no rush to leave. *Do I make it too easy for him?*

It was now dark as Larry approached the trailer. The

lights were on and he got a sinking feeling in the pit of his stomach. Then again, it would be like Colby to forget the lights on, and for once, he hoped it was the case. He lifted and moved aside the rusty screen and pulled open the glass sliding door. Colby was seated on the broken-down stained sofa which also served as his bed. His eyes were fixed on the TV screen as his hands expertly packed the bowl of his pipe with weed. The sickly-sweet stench hung heavy in the air.

"How long have you been here?" Larry questioned.

"Why? What do you care?" Colby countered and kept his attention on his pipe as he fired up his lighter and took a deep drag, squinting his eyes.

"Put that shit away. You're on parole, you jackass. And what's that on your shirt?" he asked, staring at the dark stain. Colby glanced down.

"It's ketchup."

Chapter 7

Krista

Parker Graves was the first man to show any kind of interest in Krista Chamberlain, and she was smitten. A lifetime of being awkward and getting teased, but not recognizing the jabs until she was older, had left her vulnerable and desperate. She was brilliant, and she knew it. The highest GPA in high school and a full year's worth of college credits had set her up to finish her university degree in only three years. During those three years she watched from the sidelines as the other girls flirted, dated, and socialized. With all of her academic knowledge and gifts, she couldn't crack the code of how to fit in and be a normal college girl.

When college life ended, Krista had even fewer chances

to socialize and meet people. In her company's office, she was much younger than everyone else and when colleagues included her in any social invitations, it was strictly out of obligation. No one sought her companionship on purpose. Every once in a while, her old college roommates included her when they were going out. Krista saw to this by texting one or more of them, asking what they were doing and then asking to be included. *It would be nice if just once, they would be the ones to initiate.* When she tried to host a gathering or suggest an outing, excuses were made by all and it was hard for Krista to take. With no siblings, and only her father as a close relative, she felt alone in the world.

Krista believed meeting Parker and becoming his girlfriend was the best thing ever to happen to her and she relished it. She remained blissfully unaware of red flags that a close friend, if she had one, might have pointed out. Parker kept unusual hours with his job. Krista had never been to his house. Sometimes a week would pass before he answered her texts. She wasn't pushy and never demanded an explanation. She understood that Parker was a private person. She could respect that. If he was short on cash, Krista was fine with picking up the tab, grateful to have a man, a good-looking one at that, show interest. She never asked about his allowance from his parents or his salary from his job, unsure if as his girlfriend she had a right to the information.

Parker promised to introduce her to his parents, but they were living overseas with no plans to return. He wanted to bring her home, but his roommates didn't allow guests. House rules. Sometimes his job required him to travel at unexpected times, for unspecified amounts of time. He hinted his job was top secret and for her own protection he could not give details.

There were no friends to discuss her concerns with and Krista was so thrilled to not be alone in the world, it was easier to let it slide. It was cute how Parker liked to read her texts and email. That's how he knew her plan to visit Snowy Plover Inn. Krista's relative, Charlene, had contacted her by email. Charlene's father, actually stepfather, was related to Krista's father. They were second cousins, or first removed, or something. Charlene wanted to meet her, and invited Krista to the inn for a few days or a week if she could make it. Grateful for the attention and an invitation that she didn't have to ask for, Krista accepted without reservation.

"Who is this Charlene?" Parker asked. "And why would she invite you for a vacation when you've never met? Sounds sketchy. I should go with you."

"Sure, do you think you can get some time off?" Krista played it cool and didn't want to get her hopes up. She still wasn't clear on what Parker actually did for a living, but a vacation with her boyfriend would be a dream come true. Her life was finally getting better. She asked her boss for the week off. She had never used her vacation time before, and the request was granted without question. Not knowing who was paying for what, she visited the Snowy Plover Inn website and reserved a room with a queen bed and a sitting area and private bath for the week. Then she sent Charlene a text to let her know and got an immediate response.

"That's perfect. I'm so glad you'll be able to stay all week. I'll be staying in the owner's cottage with my best friend who just bought the inn. Also, it's my treat. Again, so glad you'll make it." Krista was shocked at the woman's generosity. Twenty-one hundred would have been a stretch for her budget, but she assumed Parker would offer to pay at least some of it. She'd need to choose a suitable thank you gift for Charlene. Maybe an expensive bottle of wine; Parker would know what to buy.

Krista arrived at the inn without Parker, a day later than planned. He'd not called for a few days prior and she'd already sent a reminder. She was disappointed, but had committed to and needed a vacation, so she left without him mid-morning on what should have been the second day of her stay. The drive up the coast was beautiful. *I should get out of the city more often.*

It was 1:30 p.m. when Krista pulled up and was greeted by a friendly woman with a warm smile who introduced herself as Pearla and showed her where to park. Krista pulled into the spot, grabbed her small rolling suitcase and shoulder bag from the trunk, and paused for a moment to take in the scene. Her heart hurt a little that Parker wasn't there to share it. She pushed the thought away and went in the front double doors to the reception area where Pearla stood waiting.

"I'll just send Charlene a quick text. She'll meet us at your room. Follow me. It's not the one you booked online. Charlene wanted you to have an upgrade. Her treat."

"I'm so sorry I was delayed yesterday. It was an unavoidable work emergency," Krista said. "Please charge that to my credit card." She was concerned about taking advantage of Charlene's generosity and didn't want to make a bad first impression.

"Don't even worry about that," Pearla said. "It's all settled. Char will be thrilled you made it."

Pearla led Krista through reception and into a lounge

area where several people were gathered, then up the staircase on the right.

"Charlene insisted you stay in this room. It's got a beautiful view of the front and side of the property. Lots of windows. Lots of light." She unlocked the door using a large old-fashioned key.

"Wow! This is gorgeous," Krista gushed as she took in the room. She wasn't bothered that it was slightly on the shabby side and needed renovating.

The sheer gauzy curtains let in the early afternoon light, and the sofa was the perfect place to curl up in front of a fire. In the bathroom stood an old clawfoot tub. Bright white fluffy towels were stacked on a dresser and two robes hung on wooden pegs. Tears filled her eyes and threatened to spill, and without thinking, Krista turned to Pearla saying, "I'm alone. My boyfriend can't make it."

"Oh, honey," Pearla said. "I'm sorry to hear that, but I'm sure you'll enjoy yourself either way. Charlene is so glad you're here."

"Yes, I am," Charlene said as she stepped through the door and held out her hand, but when Krista approached, gave her a hug instead. Krista returned the warm hug and felt instantly better.

"I have so much to show you and I can't wait to get to know all about you." Char paused. "I know you just got here and might want to settle in, but there's a naturalist leading an educational bird watching walk today. He's leading it in," she checked her watch, "about 15 minutes."

"I'd love to. Let me just set my stuff down and change my shoes. I can settle in later," Krista said without hesitation.

Charlene's warm welcome and the beauty of the inn

were just the combination she needed. *I'm going to enjoy this time with or without Parker.*

She kicked off her flats and dug out her hiking shoes from the bottom of her suitcase, purposely pushing aside the silky lingerie. She checked her phone once more, before putting the notifications on silent. If Parker changed his mind, he knew where to find her.

Chapter 8

Maxine

Maxine kept her cool while the paramedics lifted and moved Rose McMartin onto the stretcher. Thankfully they'd arrived without a siren and flashing lights. *I hope the other guests haven't noticed.* Now they busied themselves with their patient, discussing her care amongst themselves in hushed voices and providing no details to Max. She stood by as they took a pulse, lifted Rose's eyelids, and placed an oxygen mask over her mouth and nose. Max noticed there was a gash on the top of Rose's head and was certain she was unconscious. Who knew if there were other injuries? Minutes later, a sheriff's patrol car pulled up in front of the inn. The man in uniform introduced himself to Pearla as Sheriff Rene Silva and asked to be shown to the scene of the accident. Pearla led him to the cellar by way of the kitchen.

Maxine heard heavy footsteps and saw the shiny black shoes descending the stairs, then tan trousers, a black duty belt with a gun in the holster, and finally the entire man. Pearla followed behind him and gasped. She was seeing the scene for the first time. The paramedics had wrapped the older woman's head with a gauze bandage, but blood was already seeping through in a dark stain. They had hooked her up to an IV, but she appeared to be unconscious and was very pale and still. The sheriff's eyes swept the room, then landed on Max. Pearla mouthed a silent, "Sorry," from behind him.

Great. Was it really necessary for him to parade through the entire property? She noticed his self-important expression and had to employ some quick inner dialog to keep calm.

"What happened here?" he asked.

"I don't exactly know, sir," Max stumbled for words. "My employee called me and said there'd been an accident. This woman is one of my guests."

"So I take it, you're the new owner?"

"Yes, I'm Maxine Egan. This is my grand opening," she sighed, realizing this was terrible for business if word got out. *Oh, please God. Don't let this woman die.*

"What was your guest doing down here in the cellar?" he asked as he squatted down to survey the area.

"I don't know why she was in the cellar. It's off-limits to guests," Maxine replied.

"I think she had a bit too much to drink during the wine and cheese reception," Pearla added helpfully. "She may have gotten lost on her way back to her room."

"That's interesting," the sheriff said. "The door is

clearly marked 'Private' though."

"Yes, it is," was all Maxine could think to say. *Why does this feel like an interrogation?*

"Was anything touched or moved?"

"I don't know. I don't think so, just the body, I mean, lady." Max heard the shakiness in her voice and tried to keep it steady. "As I said, my employee, Mr. Trawl called me, and I came right away. To be honest, I was just standing here trying to get my head around this. It's awful." Max shuddered.

"Ah, yes, Mr. Trawl," the sheriff said as if he knew him.

Max didn't want to elaborate that she'd almost been sick from the smell of blood. She'd been too scared to approach Rose McMartin, fearing she was already dead. She surely couldn't have stood there for very long. It seemed like only a few minutes before the paramedics had come and taken over and then the sheriff had shown up with Pearla.

"I should call for backup and I'll need to secure the area. No one is to come in here." He spoke with authority.

"Wait. What's happening? This is just an accident. We can clean up this mess, Sheriff. And if you don't mind, I'd rather keep this quiet. I wouldn't want to rattle my guests," Maxine said, barely containing her distress.

"Right," Pearla agreed. "I can start cleaning this mess up right away."

"The only one who really needs to know anything about this is Mrs. McMartin's husband," Maxine said and gasped when she realized no one had informed him yet. "In fact, I should go tell him right now."

"Look," said the Sheriff. "As much as you'd like to keep this quiet, it's not gonna happen. I will need to determine if this was an accident or something else."

"What do you mean something else? What else could it be?" Maxine said.

"You don't think someone would have done this intentionally, do you?" Pearla asked.

"That is what we will determine," said the sheriff with an authoritative air.

Max felt her spirit sink. This was the worst possible scenario for her new venture. It was a bad omen—and she allowed herself to consider that the inn might fail. And then what would she do?

Chapter 9

Pearla

As Pearla went around the inn to gather the guests and workers, for the first time since leaving her comfortable life and moving to Silvermist Point, she questioned if she'd made the right decision. The sheriff was adamant that no one should leave the premises.

"I'll need to speak to all guests individually. They must account for where they were for the last two hours."

Pearla had barely a moment to speak with Max, before Max took off to follow the ambulance.

"I need to see if Mrs. McMartin is okay. This is more important than monitoring the sheriff. You're in charge; be my eyes and ears."

Pearla went to fetch Walt McMartin from his room,

but as she knocked, she remembered he had ridden in the ambulance with his wife to the hospital thirty minutes away in Brookhaven. She proceeded to the next room when the door to Walt and Rose's suite opened.

"Hello, was someone knocking?" Roxanne stepped out of the doorway, her purse over one shoulder and her keys in her hand.

"Oh, sorry," Pearla said. "I was looking for Mr. McMartin. But I think he went to be with his wife." She tried to say 'wife' in a neutral tone. "I was coming to knock on your door next though. The sheriff's here, and he's planning to interview all the guests."

"What for?" Roxanne asked, looking agitated. "I need to leave. I'm going to the hospital. To support Walt."

Don't you mean Rose?

"It's Rose that was injured," Pearla said, not wanting her expression to betray her thoughts.

"I know. They're my friends. Obviously, I hope Rose is ok and not dead or anything."

Are you serious?

"Well, in any case, please head over to the lounge. The sheriff has requested the guests wait there. He'll call you in for questioning one at a time. I'm going to find the other guests."

"Okay, fine." Roxanne pushed past Pearla, shutting the door to Walt and Rose's room. "As long as he's quick about it. So much for a restful evening. First questioning by a police officer, then a hospital visit." Pearla heard her mutter under her breath, "I hate hospitals."

Pearla wanted to call Maxine. Max had been the first to be questioned so the sheriff could release her to go to the hospital. Pearla was dying to hear a replay of the conversation. This entire ordeal was an unfortunate accident with a small-town sheriff looking for ways to justify his salary, but she also really wanted to find out if Max knew anything, if there was any reason to worry. Adding to that was the concern that maybe she had made the wrong decision to leave her job and follow her friend. Moving to Silvermist Point seemed the perfect way to untangle herself from an unhealthy relationship and get a fresh start, but it was also a rash decision and Pearla had little in her savings account to sustain her if this venture should fail.

* * *

Pearla and Max had been in the staff lounge where they ate lunch every day during Pearla's break and Max's fourth period prep time when Max had first sprung the idea on her. Pearla knew the death of Max's husband had left her friend in a deep depression and with a lack of her usual zest for life. With no one else present, Max had confided in her.

"Pearla, I've done something absolutely crazy, and you're the first person I'm telling." Pearla leaned in conspiratorially.

"I'm all ears." *Let's hear the gossip.*

Max shared that she'd been up north to a place called Snowy Plover Inn for a getaway over the long weekend the month before.

"It's in Silvermist Point, just past Brookhaven. I used to go with Char when we were girls."

"Right. I remember you mentioning it. It sounded amazing."

"Well, it was just what I needed." Max took a deep breath. "And I bought it."

"Excuse me, you what?" Pearla set down her forkful of salad.

"I bought it, Pearla. I might be crazy. Do you think I'm crazy?"

"Wow. That's a lot. But, no. You are absolutely not crazy." Pearla leaned closer and whispered, "Except what about your job? The students?"

"Well," Max said. "The district offered me a 'golden handshake' last year, so I'm hoping it still stands. I'm technically old enough for early retirement and I need a change. I've been miserable without Adam, and Sawyer is practically grown and doesn't need me anymore." Max looked expectantly at Pearla.

"Oh my God, Max. You are awesome. This is awesome. It's a great idea to have a new adventure. This is just what you need. Only problem is, I'm going to miss you terribly."

"I'm hoping you won't need to miss me at all. I want you to come and help me run it. There's no one else I'd rather have. No pressure though. Only if you want to." Pearla was stunned at the offer. She had worked at Royal High since she was twenty-two. Thirteen years. Max had transferred from a junior high that same year and they'd been colleagues and friends from the start. Their fifteen-year age difference had never impacted their close friendship. But even as questions arose faster than she could ask them, Pearla knew she would accept.

Now Pearla thought about her last day at Royal. She had stood at the stainless-steel sink. She slid the last tray into the hot soapy water. Pearla grabbed the yellow sponge and plunged her gloved hands in after it for the last time. The movements were automated after years of repetition.

She wiped the plastic tray down and dunked it in the rinse tub, then stacked it on the rack to dry. As she pushed the mop across the linoleum, her hands trembled and she realized she was sweating. Her scalp itched under the hair net she'd forgotten to remove. She pulled it off her head and chucked it into the trash with the pile of uneaten food. She felt a bit like a snake shedding its skin. *Am I doing the right thing?*

"I'm out," Joelle shouted as she pushed the heavy metal door open. A burst of light temporarily blinded Pearla.

"See you tomorrow."

"No, you won't," Pearla thought. "I'll be driving north." It was easier this way. She'd put in her resignation, but decided not to tell her coworkers. She wasn't ready to explain herself and did not want to answer the questions.

Pearla could have followed Joelle out, but there were a few more details to wrap up, and she never liked to leave the space until everything was in perfect order. Once she rolled the big trash can out to the dumpster, she pulled off her tan over-the-head apron and hung it on the hook. She stared for a moment at the Royal High Cougar emblazoned on the front. Next, she emptied her locker and strode to the parking lot with more confidence than she felt. This was harder than she expected.

"Hey, Ms. Beckett," it was one of the football players, Cam or Chris, she didn't remember which, giving her a wave. "Have a nice day," he said. *Some kids still had manners.* If she was honest, none of the students had ever been disrespectful to her; they saved that for each other or for the teachers. Pearla got into her car and drove home to finish packing.

* * *

Now she was heading to Mr. Trawl's trailer. The other guests were gathered in the lounge and were being interviewed by the sheriff. Max said the groundskeeper was the one who called her, the first one to find Rose McMartin after the accident. *Why had he left before the sheriff arrived?* Pearla understood that he and his son were the caretakers at the inn, responsible for maintenance and landscaping and other odd jobs. Truthfully, they both gave her the willies. She wondered if they resented her arrival with Max and the fact that she was given the small studio apartment above reception rather than them.

As she passed the pavilion, Pearla was looking down at her phone, hoping for a message from Max, when Mr. Trawl startled her. He was heading in her direction.

"Oh, hi Mr. Trawl."

He interrupted.

"It's Larry. Remember?"

"Sure, yes, sorry. I was just on my way to find you. The sheriff is here and wants to have a word with everyone on the property. It's regarding the accident with the guest." He kept walking past without acknowledging her.

"Mr. Trawl, Larry, did you hear me? The sheriff's in the lounge."

"Yeah, I heard. I'll head over."

"Oh, also, can you let your son know, too?" He stopped walking.

"My son? Why?"

"He wants to speak with everyone," Pearla said. *Why does this guy have to make it weird?*

"Well, Colby's not here. He's been gone all day, left this morning, and still isn't back," he called over his shoulder.

"Oh, okay then. Just let the sheriff know."

Chapter 10

Maxine

Maxine drove the thirty minutes to the hospital alone and in silence. She hated hospitals and the memories they invoked. Char had stayed back. She wanted a chance to get to know Krista and so far their time together had been filled with activity and no real down time. Plus, this business with the accident. Max understood. She pulled up to the visitors' parking lot of Brookhaven Hospital. Max had seen enough of the insides of hospitals and doctors' offices to last her a lifetime.

Adam's diagnosis had been sudden and unexpected. They were willing to try any options to clear the cancer, but none had worked. Each time Adam had a scan, the cancer had progressed and had spread aggressively. Max remembered hearing that word and knowing immediately she would forever associate it with Adam's cancer. Until the end of his too-short life, they held fast to hope for a miracle, but Adam's six-foot-two frame continued to shrivel and waste away. He spent his last few days at home in the living room under the watchful care of 24-hour hospice nurses.

The entire ordeal took under a year. When he passed, Max was gutted. She went on about her regular life like an automaton. Sawyer took a semester off from college when his father was first diagnosed, but had returned to school at Adam's insistence. Maxine thought it might be easier for him to be away and not have to witness his father's rapid deterioration. Sawyer took his father's death hard, finding it challenging to focus on academics, and he offered to quit school again and move back home with his mom. Max wouldn't allow it.

"It will only make it harder," she'd said. "Focus on school. You know that's what Dad would have wanted for you."

It killed her to say it. She needed Sawyer near her. She wanted to have him close, but she let him go. The house felt too big with only her and Butters. Before buying the inn, she had planned to downsize, maybe a condo, but she hadn't yet begun to look.

Pushing the visceral memories aside, Max grabbed her purse and went in the visitor's entrance of Brookhaven Emergency Room to inquire about Rose McMartin.

"She's checked in and under observation. It's family only," Max was told. Still, she went up to the floor hoping to find Walt McMartin and offer some words of comfort. It was the right thing to do. He wasn't in the waiting area.

She asked the nurse on duty, "Have you seen Mr. Walt McMartin?"

"Do you know him?" the nurse asked.

"Not personally, no. He's a guest at my inn, The Snowy Plover. His wife had an accident. I wanted to check on her, and him, see how they're both doing. It was pretty traumatic, honestly," Max said.

"Well, he's an interesting man, let's say," the nurse gave a quick look around and lowered her voice. "It's none of my business, but he doesn't strike me as a grieving husband. In fact, there's not much concern at all. He was allowed to ride in the ambulance with his wife and five minutes after he got here, he asked how much an Uber would cost to get back to Silvermist Point." Max's eyebrows shot up. *Wow. Just wow.*

"How is Rose McMartin? Her injury looked serious," Max said.

"I'm sorry, but I can't give you any specific information about a patient, except to say she's in a serious condition" the nurse said.

Max thanked the nurse and headed to the cafeteria, hoping for a chance to speak with Walt. She found him huddled at a table, a Styrofoam cup of coffee and a partially eaten sandwich in front of him. He was on his phone and his mannerisms suggested the conversation was intense. Max stood back and watched, waiting for him to finish the call, before approaching. Just as he put down his phone and ran a hand through his hair, he glanced up and smiled. His eyes were fixed across the room. Following his gaze, Max saw Roxanne striding towards him in too-tight pants and kitten heels. Max quickly moved out of their sightline, but watched the interaction. *Okay, so it's not really unusual that a close friend would show up at the hospital.* But something didn't sit right.

Max knew Roxanne was a friend, but she, along with every guest, had also witnessed her shameless and relentless flirting with Walt. Walt stood and took Roxanne's hand and lightly kissed it, ever the gentleman. She came in close for a tight full-frontal hug. *Was he groping her behind? Totally inappropriate!* Max struggled to process what she saw. Were these two having an affair right under the nose of the wife? The thought sickened her, and then the next thought even more so. Would one or both of them try to harm Rose? It was too far-fetched. The poor woman had too much to drink and had suffered a fall. No one was trying to murder her. Still, Max held back and did not approach Walt and Roxanne. *They don't need to know I'm here.*

The situation was making her paranoid. There was no reason for the sheriff to blow it out of proportion. He certainly didn't need to be questioning her guests. While it was completely distasteful that Rose McMartin's husband and her friend were likely having an affair, it wasn't a reason to kill her. *It would honestly make more sense if Rose tried to kill one of them.* Maxine dialed Charlene, hoping to get information about what happened after she left. Thankfully, Char picked up.

"Hey Char, what's going on over there? Did the sheriff question everyone?"

"He gathered everyone in the lounge and then had us write exactly where we were and what we were doing from 5:30 p.m. to 7:15 p.m. I was first to hand mine in. I swear, Max, it felt like I was back in school. He read it over and dismissed me without question; Krista too. We're gonna head to the village and get dinner and a drink at Barnaby's.

I want to see the owner for myself. Meet us there?"

"I'm still at the hospital. Mrs. McMartin is in serious, but stable condition. The nurse wouldn't tell me much. I'm going to try to visit with her, if they'll let me." Max ended the conversation and headed back upstairs. She was encouraged to find a different staff member on duty.

"I'd like to see Rose McMartin, please." The young man looked up from his phone. "Sure, go ahead." Max obeyed before he could change his mind or read Rose McMartin's chart. She moved quickly and closed the door softly behind her. Rose's eyes were closed, and she did not look well. Max reached out and touched her hand.

"Rose, it's Maxine Egan, the new owner of the inn. I came to check on you. I hope you're feeling better." *Best to keep it optimistic.* Rose's eyes fluttered open and Max felt the woman squeeze her hand.

"What is it?" Max asked. "Should I get the nurse or call your husband?"

Rose's eyes grew wide, then darted around the room, and she said in a raspy yet clear voice, "No."

"Is there something you want to tell me, Rose?"

"No accident." Maxine watched as her eyes fluttered and closed.

Panicking, she turned toward the door, intending to get the nurse. Through the window, she saw Walt and Roxanne coming towards the room, and quickly concealed herself behind the curtain surrounding the other bed next to Rose. Max sat on the empty bed and pulled up her feet just as Walt and Roxanne entered, careful not to move and crunch the plastic mattress cover. The curtain was sheer enough to make out shapes. She sat stock still. Walt and Roxanne had their backs to Max and were facing Rose. They were only a few feet away. *What will they think if they discover me hiding here? Why AM I hiding?*

"Looks like she's still out cold," Roxanne said with a sniff.

"Do you think she'll remember anything?" Walt asked.

"I doubt it. She was knocked hard with that can and with the fall she probably hit her head again on the cement floor. I think she lost a lot of blood, too. This might be goodbye. For good."

"Hand me that pillow," Walt said. "I want to make sure she's extra comfortable." *Was that sarcasm? What an ass!*

"It's nice and dense," Roxanne said. Max saw Walt's shape through the curtain as he held up the pillow and… *was he about to smother his wife?* She wasn't sure what she was seeing, but Walt was bent over the head of the bed and it looked like his arms were straight and pushing down the pillow. Rose kicked out her legs and began to thrash. Then the door opened, and the nurse entered.

"Hey there. I came to check the patient's…" he glanced at the chart in his hands, "Rose McMartin's vitals."

"Sure. I was just making her comfortable." Walt cleared his throat and stood up straight, backing away from the bed.

"Oh, no, sir. You cannot be touching the patient! She has a head injury! You could do damage!" The nurse was flustered.

"Also, you need to step out for a minute. Now! She's not supposed to have any visitors, not until she's stable."

"Okay, okay, we're leaving," Roxanne said as they exited the room. Max stayed still, listening as the nurse spoke to himself.

"Crap. Hopefully, no one saw that I let them in. I do

not need to get fired." Max patiently waited for him to leave before sneaking out while offering a silent prayer that Rose would be okay. *Then you can leave your husband. He doesn't deserve you.*

Chapter 11

Sheriff Rene Silva

Once Sheriff Silva cleared the cellar of people, he surveyed and photographed the scene with a critical eye. Blood was smeared everywhere in an attempt to clean it up. Head injuries always bled profusely. The owner, Maxine, said she hadn't touched a thing. So who had moved the body before help arrived, who had moved the oil can, and why? The sheriff was fairly certain it was all coincidence and an accident, but he was bored and needed a bit of excitement in his life. For this reason, he liked to follow the 911 calls, especially if there was an injury involved. Plus, he didn't want his investigative skills to get rusty. He'd moved to this small enclave thinking the slow pace would be good for him, less stressful. Turns out, he enjoyed and missed the fast-paced and dangerous life as an L.A. police officer. *If only I hadn't messed up so bad.*

There were two incidents that had compelled Silva to leave his job or else face public humiliation. That one time when he'd allegedly used too much force handling a perpetrator who turned out to be a minor celebrity and the other time he'd been accused of mishandling evidence pertinent to a case. Both were bullshit and neither resulted in any actual disciplinary measures. However, the higher-ups lorded the incidents over him with veiled threats that they could come to light if necessary and wouldn't he be happier and better off seeking opportunities elsewhere? No, he wouldn't, thank you very much. But, he had jumped at the chance to leave L.A. when the position at Silvermist Point opened up.

His job title of Sheriff for Silvermist Point meant that he was his own boss. No one was paying attention to the goings-on here, and more importantly, no one tried to micro-manage him. Silvermist was tiny and everyone knew everyone else, or so it seemed. Being naturally suspicious, he'd bristled at the invitation to meet the townspeople at get-togethers or take part in any community events. He wasn't used to being included in social activities and thought, for sure, anyone who offered an invitation must have an ulterior motive. No way was it genuine. June would mark his one-year anniversary of coming to Silvermist and he was settling in and believing that maybe the folks here were as true as they seemed.

Gathering the guests at the inn was the prudent move. He was only fulfilling his duty. He'd talk to them, then let them go. Write up a report, and be done. A clumsy old lady fell. That was all this was. *But why had there been so much movement at the scene?* He was curious to speak with Mr. Trawl who was first to find the victim. *Lady, not a victim.* He'd already met the son, Colby, several times, and was in touch with his parole officer who checked in once a month. Their last encounter involved Colby urinating in public. He'd argued that since no "public" was around, it shouldn't be considered public urination and Rene Silva had let him go with a warning. Colby had grown up in Silvermist and was affectionately known as one of the town's local ne'er-do-wells. People pitied him. Rene thought of the numerous petty thieves, criminals, junkies, and gang members he'd had to deal with on the daily in L.A. Colby Trawl was lucky to be here in a town where people knew and tolerated him. *He doesn't know how easy he has it.*

What about the owner? Maxine Egan had left the scene without being officially excused, even though she had offered a quick statement, and this bothered him. She claimed she was in her cottage at the time of the call from Larry Trawl, the maintenance man, which came through at 6:42 p.m.

"Here's my number. We can talk later. I've got to get to the hospital. Please direct your questions to Pearla Beckett. She's the manager." Maxine had handed him her business card and left. It didn't matter. She had no reason to purposely injure a guest, this he knew for certain.

By speaking with Pearla, Rene Silva gathered the time of the incident was between 5 and 6:40 pm. There had been a wine and cheese reception in the lounge area and the following guests and staff were in attendance: Rose McMartin, Walt McMartin, Roxanne Whitam, Maxine Egan, Charlene Thomas, Krista Chamberlain, Keith Lombard, and M. Singer. Pearla Beckett was in and out. Larry Trawl was gardening and doing maintenance, up until noticing the cellar door ajar, when he entered and discovered the injured older lady.

After interviewing the guests, with the exception of Walt McMartin, who had ridden with his wife in the ambulance, and after reviewing his notes, Rene Silva surmised everyone technically had the opportunity to be in the cellar to injure Rose McMartin. No guest could corroborate any other guests' whereabouts. Apparently, all were alone at the approximate time of the incident. Frustrating. Larry Trawl had explained with a flustered apology that he was only trying to help the lady by wiping up blood and moving her into a more comfortable position.

"I was in shock when I found her," he said. "That's the last thing I expected to see. I wasn't thinking straight, and I called the owner and 911 right away. This is not good for the inn. I hope I don't lose my job because of this."

Larry Trawl seemed sincere enough to Rene Silva, as did all the guests. There was some suggestion that all was not well regarding the McMartins' marriage, but that was only hearsay. After all, the husband was with her in the ambulance. He obviously cared for his wife. Sheriff Silva would prefer to definitively conclude that the incident was an accident, and believed he had enough evidence to call the investigation over. Besides, he was supposed to be off duty now. He did not appreciate working more than a regular day and didn't care about racking up overtime. He was long overdue for his nightly gin and tonic or a glass of wine. Earl would be ornery about not being served his meal promptly at 5:30. *I hope he doesn't pee on my slippers again.* Plus, he'd missed the six o'clock news.

Chapter 12

Pearla

Pearla stayed nearby, flitting from the reception area to the lounge to the kitchen to the walk-in pantry and back while trying to look busy. Sheriff Silva was conducting his interviews in the private office connected to the reception area. The guests were assembled in the lounge awaiting his directive. He first asked all who were present to write down exactly where they were and what they were doing between 5 p.m. and 7 p.m. He handed out small pads and pens with the Snowy Plover Inn logo he'd grabbed from the office. "I'll call you in individually. Until then, stay here, please."

Pearla was a crime fan. She devoured fiction and non-fiction mysteries through books, podcasts and documentaries. As she watched, listened, or read, she often jotted down pertinent information to see if she could solve the puzzle or guess who the perpetrator was. But this mystery felt too close to home. She wanted to believe it was an unfortunate accident, but when she observed the scene in the wine cellar, she was all but certain it was not.

Drawing on her extensive crime knowledge base, Pearla surmised there was no way the oil container could fall in the manner suggested. The shelf where the oil was stocked had a three-inch lip. The can would have had to be pushed in order to knock out the lady. It was no accident. Still, she kept her mouth shut. *I'll keep my theories to myself.* It wasn't her business to get mixed up in this type of drama. No good would come of it. Rose McMartin wasn't dead, so it's not as if this was a murder. Obviously, her despicable husband and/or so-called best friend might want Rose dead. And distasteful as it was, Rose would need to deal with it when she woke. It was not her business, Pearla decided. This was a situation best handled by a competent divorce attorney.

Larry Trawl's demeanor was troubling though. When he'd been given the pad and pen, he looked all around like, "What am I supposed to do with this?" Trying to be helpful, Pearla reminded him to write where he was and what he'd been doing between 5 p.m. and 7 p.m. as Sheriff Silva requested.

"I'm not gonna frickin' write stuff down. If he wants to know, he can ask me." Larry slammed the pad and pen down on a side table and headed for the door. "I'll be outside. Or in my trailer."

Had he emphasized *trailer*? Pearla still held a little guilt regarding moving into the studio apartment over the reception area of the inn. Did Larry want it for himself? He was a long-time employee at the inn, and who would like living in a trailer? Max had never considered allowing him to move into the apartment though, and she wouldn't. She'd kept him on as maintenance man as a favor to the previous owners and owed him nothing. Besides, his son, Colby, was a creep. Colby was closer in age to Max and had attempted to flirt with Pearla the first time she ran into him. She'd made it clear she wasn't interested. *What is it about me that I attract such losers?*

Pearla was last to be called into the office, right after Larry Trawl, who walked out with his face more screwed up in anger than usual. The man never looked pleasant. *It must be tiring carrying such a large chip on your shoulder, and sporting a permanent resting bitch face.* She was nervous. The sheriff was a large man, intimidating, and her experience with law enforcement wasn't positive. The law had let her down when she'd sought help before. It took three tries before police granted a restraining order, requiring her former boyfriend to stay at least twenty-five feet from her. She touched the small scar above her lip. She tried to push that thought away and focus on the present.

"How can I be of help?" She sat down across from the sheriff who had pulled the chair from the desk over to the round conference table.

"Let's begin with where you were during the hours in question. I see you wrote, 'in and out of the living room, reception, kitchen, office, and my apartment.' Is that accurate? And can you be more specific?"

"I'll try. I'm trying to recall who was present and when they left the reception, particularly Mrs. McMartin. But, as I wrote down, I was in and out of the room."

"I see," the sheriff said, but he looked expectantly at Pearla, waiting for more.

"I began clearing the food and drinks at about 5:40-

5:45. Maxine was going to check something in the office and was then going home to her cottage. It's on the premises. Charlene said she was taking a walk and after, planned to head over to meet Max at the cottage. She's staying there. Her cousin, Krista, was choosing a book to take back to her room. Krista's in the upstairs suite. I know all three were meeting later to go to dinner in town at Barnaby's."

"And what about the other guests?"

"Ms. Singer wasn't in the living room when I cleared the food, so she must have left before then, but I didn't see her go. Walt and Roxanne, that's Mr. McMartin and Ms. Whitam, left earlier than that, probably around five-fifteen. Roxanne left first, and Walt maybe five minutes after." Without thinking, Pearla added, "There was a little dust-up between those two and Mrs. McMartin." That got the Sheriff's attention.

"Explain what you mean by dust-up." Too late. *Crap. Why did I say that? It's none of my business.* Pearla wanted to take back the words.

"It's not my place to say, but the three of them aren't getting along. There was some tension." *Oh, God. I'm making it worse.*

"I see," Sheriff Silva said. He was writing notes on a yellow legal pad.

"So the only guests in the living room after 5:45 p.m. were Rose McMartin and Keith Lombard. I didn't come back after that. I cleaned up the kitchen, then went upstairs to my apartment."

"What were you doing in your apartment?" *You can't be serious.*

"I was out on the deck, the widow's walk, and then I was finishing a movie I started earlier." *And enjoying a glass of wine, not that it's any of your business.*

"When were you last in the wine cellar?"

"I was in the cellar earlier today when I gave Ms. Singer a tour of the property. That was when the other guests went on a guided nature walk to the shore, so maybe two or two-thirty. And again, at about 4:15 to grab some wine for the reception."

"And Mr. Trawl? Was he down there earlier in the day that you know of? Or his son?" *Where is he going with this?*

"I'm not sure." When it was clear Pearla wasn't going to elaborate, the Sheriff asked, "Any thoughts on what Mr. Trawl was doing in the cellar when he found Mrs. McMartin?"

"Not really, no. Did you ask him?" This seemed to catch the sheriff off guard, but he recovered quickly.

"I did ask him, but I'm asking you too."

"Sure, of course. Let's see." Pearla considered her words. She had no reason to be nervous, but she couldn't help but feel like she was in the principal's office getting grilled about the behavior of the bad kids, and she wanted no part of it.

"We had a delivery come in earlier, some dishes and linens. They were in the office. Maxine leaves the Trawls notes in the utility shed regarding tasks she wants done. I know she wanted the boxes moved to the wine cellar." Pearla met the sheriff's eyes. "Maybe he was moving the boxes." After a beat, she added, "Or checking that his son moved them."

"Tell me. Did you notice they were already there when you followed me down the stairs? The boxes, I mean. I assume you're referring to the boxes of dishes someone pushed to the side, away from the blood." This felt like a game of cat and mouse. Pearla didn't feel like it was she that the sheriff was after, but he thought she knew something. And the sheriff was trying to get at it without asking her outright. Well, she wasn't going to play. He'd need to ask directly. And then he did.

"Were you in the cellar before I got here, but after four-fifteen?" Sheriff Silva asked.

"No," Pearla said. There was a brief pause as Sheriff Silva scribbled on his pad. Then he stood. Pearla stood too, facing him and noticing the details of him for the first time. She'd been too distracted before. He was about five-foot-ten and husky with a short military style haircut and prominent eyebrows. His mustache and goatee were impeccably groomed. Pearla stood straight with her shoulders back. She was only five-foot-three, but met his eyes, hers unblinking. He cracked a huge smile and held out his hand. *What is happening right now?*

"Pearla, Ms. Beckett. It's been a pleasure to meet you. I'm sorry it's under these stressful circumstances." She shook his hand and cautiously returned the smile.

"Thank you, Sheriff. Let us know if you need anything else."

"Okay, I'll do that. I may be back tomorrow with one of my deputies to have a look around. I'll check in at the hospital too. I'd like to ask Mrs. McMartin some questions once she's up to it."

As he was walking out, Pearla thought to ask, "Is it okay if I clean up down in the cellar?"

"Yes. That should be fine," he said.

She watched the patrol car pull away, then took her phone from her back pocket and called Max. She picked up on the first ring.

"Hey, Pearla, I'm driving back to town. What's happening over there?"

"Everything's fine. The sheriff just left. He interviewed everyone and said I could clean up. How's Rose McMartin?"

"She's fine for now. I saw the husband at the hospital. Roxanne showed up too. Pearla, this whole thing is so weird. I think they're having an affair. It seems crazy they'd try to hurt Rose though, or kill her. What does the sheriff think? It was an accident, right?" Max asked hopefully.

"It's hard to say what he thinks. He's impossible to read. At first, he was kinda being a jerk, but then he was nice and friendly before he left."

"Did Char and Krista leave yet? Can you get a ride with them to Barnaby's? I want you to join us."

"They left, but I'm gonna stay here and clean up the mess, put everything back in order."

"Are you sure? I can have the Trawls do that tomorrow. Come meet us."

"No, but thanks. I'm beat and I don't feel like changing clothes."

"Okay, then. I'll see you in the morning. Come over with Krista for breakfast."

"That should be fine, after I set up the morning breakfast spread."

"Sounds good," Max said. Pearla hung up.

Pearla went to the supply closet and grabbed a bucket, mop, rubber gloves and bleach. She planned to clean the cellar thoroughly. She opened the door from the kitchen and flicked the light switch. The smell of blood assaulted her nose. She got to work cleaning and bleaching, grateful the floor was concrete and not carpeted. She wiped down all the metal shelving and put everything back in order.

Deciding the bloody dish towels were unsalvageable, she tossed them in a trash bag and tied the top. The boxes that had gotten blood on the bottom, she emptied and flattened.

Then she carried and stacked the new dishes on the counter under the kitchen cabinets upstairs. They would need to be washed. The linens, she put on the shelf in the cellar. She took the trash to the dumpster near the utility shed and returned to the wine cellar from the outside door. When everything was in place, she went back out the upstairs door and then came back in taking each stair slowly. She'd returned the cleaned-off oil can to the top metal shelf and now she stared up at it. She grabbed the metal shelf as she stood on the stairs and pulled it, then shook it vigorously. The metal oil container slid a few inches sideways, but did not tip over the ledge. She shook the shelf again, more forcefully, and then the can fell. On the other side of the shelf. Not toward the stairs. *Just as I thought.*

She went to the bottom of the stairs and around the left side to face the front of the metal shelf. She picked up the oil can and reached on tiptoes to return it to the top shelf. Next, she tried to push it from where she stood. She wasn't tall enough, but there was a wooden step ladder against the wall. Standing on the second rung, she reached up and pushed the can again, this time with force. It tipped over the three-inch ledge, off the shelf, and landed on the second to last stair, then tumbled off. The two-gallon can was only half full now. A lot had spilled out earlier. Had someone deliberately pushed the full container intending to hurt or kill Rose McMartin? *Seems plausible, but who and why?*

Pearla returned the container to the shelf once again and sat on the top of the small step ladder. She heard the outside door open with a creak and felt a gush of nighttime air. Colby Trawl stood in the doorway. He looked surprised to see her. She stood.

"What are you doing here, Colby? Mr. Trawl?" He hesitated.

"I heard there was a mess to clean up, so I came to do it." *Where would he have heard that?*

"Already done. I took care of it," Pearla said.

Colby looked around and sniffed the air. "Good. You used bleach. That'll take the blood smell right out."

Pearla didn't know what to say. Her mind was going all kinds of places, none good.

"I'll go then," Colby said, eyeing her up and down with a strange half-smile before turning to leave.

"Good night," Pearla said, trying to keep her voice level. When he walked away, she waited, rubbing her arms as her skin prickled with goosebumps. Then she bolted the door. *Silly, I suppose, since he has a key.*

Chapter 13

Maxine

Maxine arrived at Barnaby's and parked her car in the lot near the back entrance. Once inside, she let her eyes adjust to the low lighting, then scanned the room for Char and Krista. She saw them at a corner booth, sitting across from each other. Catching Charlene's eye, she signaled she was going to the bar to get a drink.

"I'll join you in a minute," she called as she made her way to an empty stool at the end of the bar. Tyne Barnaby noticed her and came over. She leaned forward and asked quietly, "What can you tell me about Sheriff Rene Silva?"

"Well, hello to you, too," he joked, leaning on his elbows across from her, his dark wavy hair tousled and looking like it needed a trim. Maxine was distracted for a second. *Oh my gosh, stop. Focus.*

"Oh, sorry. I guess you haven't heard the gossip yet. I thought it might've spread by now, small town and all." Maxine tried not to show her exasperation.

"No, I've heard it, to be sure. Exciting stuff for our little village."

Max wondered what he'd heard, but wasn't sure how to ask.

"So tell me about Rene Silva." Max figured she could spend a few minutes chatting before joining Char and Krista in the booth. Tyne leaned closer and Max got a whiff of his cologne.

"Well, he's our assigned sheriff and there's not much to 'sheriff' around here, if you know what I mean, so he enjoys creating some drama from time to time," Tyne said without offering more detail.

"Great. The inn is the star of the newest drama then. I'm afraid to ask what you've heard, but what have you heard?" There. It was out.

"I heard one of your guests got injured. It's all the buzz in the village. 'Under suspicious circumstances.' Is there any truth to that?"

Maxine audibly sighed. She wanted to roll her eyes, but stopped herself.

"Very little. An older lady took a spill. End of story, as far as I can see, but Sheriff Silva claims there might be more to it. He's acting very official."

"He would," Tyne replied and pushed a short glass of cold beer across the bar to Maxine. "Here, try this sample. Local brewery."

"Thanks," she said, and took a swig. "He gathered all my guests into the lounge then pulled them one at a time for questioning. The whole experience is very awkward. It's my grand opening for goodness sake!" Max looked into Tyne's eyes. "He said he was calling for backup and taped off the area as an actual crime scene to collect evidence."

"Not sure what back-up he called," Tyne said. "Silva is a one man show. I mean obviously if there was something big happening, other law enforcement would come from Brookhaven, but for all other matters, it's him alone. It's funny he said that. Probably wants to sound important and official. He came from the LAPD."

"That's quite a change," Max said. "I wonder why he left."

"Oh, believe me, there are theories. But that's all just gossip. I think he's a good guy. We're lucky to have a designated sheriff at all. He wasn't too friendly at first, but I'd say he's warming up. He just joined us last year. I'm sure this business with the inn will all blow over soon."

"That's good to know. Thanks." Maxine stood and pushed in the stool.

"Wait, what else can I get you? Did you like the sample?"

"It was good, but I'm in the mood for a Whiskey Sour. And an order of garlic fries, please."

"I'll have the server bring them over to the table in a few."

"Come join us if you get a free minute. I want to introduce you to my friend, Charlene, and her cousin." Max hoped she wasn't being too forward, but she liked him. She couldn't help herself.

"Will do," he said and winked.

Max joined Char and Krista at the table. She quickly relayed her experience at the hospital then paused, waiting expectantly. Both ladies sat in silence for a minute before

Krista spoke up.

"Do you think it was foul play? The husband and that friend seem awfully suspicious." Max felt the same, but the whole thing was so far-fetched and too obvious. But, before she could respond, Tyne showed up with an enormous plate of garlic fries and her drink. Placing the fries in the center of the table and setting Max's drink down on a coaster, he introduced himself.

"I'm Tyne Barnaby, the proud owner of this hole-in-the-wall, and you must be Charlene and Krista. Max told me you were coming." *He sounds like we're old friends.*

"Those smell heavenly!" Char reached over and plucked a french fry from the platter. "Never mind that I've already eaten a huge dinner. I couldn't wait. It's nice to meet you, Tyne." Char kicked Max softly under the table.

"You never can," Max said.

"Dig in," Tyne laughed. "These are one of our specialties. Can I get you ladies another drink?" Krista ordered a coffee and Char, another beer. When Tyne left, Char let out a low whistle.

"Wow, Max. You weren't kidding." Krista giggled.

Max raised her eyebrows and said, "I know, but let's get back to what's important. What happened after I left? What did the sheriff ask you?"

"He was laser focused on when each guest left the living room. I tried to help pinpoint the time exactly, but it's not as if I was checking my watch. I didn't even have my phone with me; it was silenced and in my room. I told him I left when the wine and cheese reception was wrapping up. Pearla had just asked if anyone wanted anything else. It was soon after you and Char took off, then I chose a book for later," Krista said. "After that, I was relaxing in my room. I never even heard the ambulance."

"They didn't have the siren on. Neither did the sheriff," Max said. "What about you, Char?"

"I didn't have my phone either, so I couldn't provide the exact time when I left the living room. I was out walking the grounds for a bit before going to the cottage to shower and that must be when you got the call from Mr. Trawl."

"Right," Max said. "Did the sheriff seem concerned?"

"No, not really. I feel like he was just going through the motions. You know, just acting official," Char concluded.

"Okay, different subject. Krista, tell us about your boyfriend. Do you think he'll be able to join you this week?"

Krista told her new friend, Max, and newly met relative, Charlene, all about Parker. She was careful to cast him in the most positive light, upselling his good looks and downplaying his sometimes lack of consideration.

Chapter 14

Monday
Krista

Krista woke to a ping on her phone, surprised at the light in the room. She'd slept deeply and hadn't woken up once during the night. She snuggled further into the warm cocoon of a linen sheet-wrapped comforter, then looked over at the digital clock. It read, 7:13. She hadn't bothered setting the alarm. Too early, she thought. She never allowed herself to sleep in and was enjoying the feeling of not getting up to go to work as she normally would on a Monday. By now, she would have checked her emails and responded to any urgent ones, had a coffee or two, done a yoga routine, and been ready to leave for work, arriving before anyone else, as always. First there and last to leave. *And all for what?*

At the sound of the second ping, she came out of the coziness, grabbed the robe off the chair, and slid into her fuzzy slippers. Her phone was charging on the bathroom counter where she'd left it with the sound on, hoping for a message from Parker. She picked it up and tapped the screen. Call me, Parker had texted. Krista busied herself for a full fifteen minutes before returning the call.

She infused her voice with nonchalance when he answered on the first ring.

"Hey, how's it going?" Parker asked casually as if he hadn't been MIA since Thursday.

"It's fine. Great actually. It's very beautiful here." Krista would not ask if he was planning to show up. She would not ask where he was. She refused to provide anything but brief responses with no details. He'd already caused her to miss out on Saturday and she was over getting her hopes up.

"I thought I might make it up there today or tomorrow." *Do not let him hear your emotion.*

"Sure, whatever you want," Krista was pleased with herself, "I'm heading to breakfast now. I'll probably go into the village to explore later, so just let me know if you plan to show up."

"Oh, okay." Parker sounded thrown off by her words. "How's your relative? Charlene, is it?" *You know it is. What happened to all your concerns from before?*

"She's really nice." Krista purposely kept her answers short. She was not keen to forgive Parker for ditching her just yet.

"Well, I'll let you know if I'm coming."

"Great. You do that. Bye." She hung up and slowly unclenched her left fist, noticing the nail marks in her palm. Krista was angry and frustrated, but proud that in a small way, she had stood up to Parker. At the very least, she hadn't let him get to her. Today she would think only of herself. She wanted to explore the grounds, go back down to the beach, read, go in the pool. There was plenty to keep her occupied, and the slow pace was good for her, just what she needed from her too-busy life. Charlene was easy to talk to, so open and friendly. Krista said a quick prayer of thanks for meeting her and jotted down Charlene's name in her gratitude journal along with, "Snowy Plover Inn" and "time for myself".

Krista made her bed and put her room in order, then went downstairs for coffee and something to eat. The living room was inviting, with the fireplace going and the smell of fresh coffee and cinnamon. Professor Lombard glanced up from his tablet and said hello. Krista responded and made eye contact with him, then with the romance writer whose name she had forgotten. She sensed that neither was interested in conversation and the familiar feeling of being left out and awkward threatened her good mood. She busied herself preparing her coffee to the perfect shade of light beige, and was deciding what to eat and where to sit when Pearla came in from the kitchen.

"I'm glad I caught you. Char didn't want to wake you, but asked me to tell you to head over to the cottage if you like. She wasn't sure when you'd be up. I'm happy to walk you over."

"Alright. Should I fix a plate first?"

"No need, unless there's a specific pastry that's caught your eye. They're making omelets. Here, I'll carry that for you." Pearla held out a hand to take the mug from her. Krista gave it over then took a napkin and wrapped up an almond bear claw.

"I don't think I can resist this," she said smiling. "It'll pair well with an omelet."

"Absolutely!" Pearla agreed.

The two women left through the French doors and took the path to Maxine's cottage.

"So what do you think of the inn so far?" Pearla asked.

"It's magical, I love it. I haven't slept that well in … I can't remember," Krista answered.

"And who is this?" she asked as a large cream tabby appeared from out of the lilac bushes lining the path. Krista knelt down to greet the friendly cat who graciously rubbed his snout against her outstretched palm.

"That's Butters. Resident Feline Extraordinaire," Pearla said. "The Snowy Plover Inn fits his lifestyle just fine."

"Will he let me pick him up, do you think?" Krista was scooping up the cat before Pearla could answer. She put her face close, and Butters gave her a lick on the nose and purred loudly.

"Let's bring him inside," Pearla said when they reached Max's cottage. "He's not supposed to be wandering off. Max will be glad you found him."

The stone cottage was straight out of a fairy tale. It was styled differently than the inn, but Krista liked it just as much. Noticing the basket of shoes, Krista kicked off her own before proceeding in. Pearla did the same.

"Grab some slippers if you like," Max called. Inside, Krista saw Max had personalized the cottage with botanical art prints, candles and potted plants. Char greeted her warmly and she took a seat at the rough plank wooden table near the kitchen area.

"Anything I can do to help?" Krista asked.

"No, no, just make yourself at home," Max said. Krista glanced around, noticing the cottage was an open concept style with the fireplace, living room kitchen and dining area all flowing together, yet distinctly separate. Krista saw a steep narrow set of stairs leading to a loft area which took up half the ceiling space. The rest of the main room had a twenty-foot knotty pine ceiling supported by thick oak beams. Krista could see why Max bought the inn and was once again grateful to get to experience it.

"How would you like your omelet? We have spinach, cheddar, feta, mushrooms and pancetta," Max said.

"Ooh, a little of everything, please. I can't decide," Krista said, unused to anyone making her a custom breakfast. When the omelets were done, Max brought them to the table and the women sat down and dug in.

"I hope today will be more restful for you. That was a lot yesterday. My first ever guests and someone ends up hospitalized," Max said, taking a bite.

"Yeah, about that," Pearla said. "I don't think it was an accident. I did a bit of experimenting last night while cleaning up and I just don't see any possible way that container of oil could have fallen on Rose McMartin and injured her like that. No matter how drunk she was." She let that sink in, while she took a bite and chewed before adding, "Max, that information stays here. I will do nothing with it. I have no plans to call the sheriff and I don't believe he suspects a thing. All those interviews were just procedural. He let me clean it all up so there's really no evidence. I just thought you should know."

Max slid her plate forward, rested her chin on her hands, and sighed. Char, Pearla, and Krista waited. No one wanted to respond. Char was first to speak.

"Well, I'm certainly not saying a thing."

"Me neither," Krista agreed, feeling honored to be included. *I'll pretend I never heard that. No way I'd jeopardize my new friends.*

"Okay, good," Max finally said. "Let's not call the sheriff. There's no point. He obviously has no leads, anyway. Pearla, any theories on who did it or why?"

"Doesn't it have to be Roxanne or Walt? Who else has a motive?" Charlene asked.

"But that just seems so obvious. Too obvious," Krista said. The women sat in silence for a moment until all four sat taller and looked around.

"Did you all feel that? Or was it just me?" Max asked. *I felt it, but what was it?*

"It feels like something passed through here. I just got the chills. Is that what you mean?" Krista said.

"I was wondering if she was still here, or if she'd moved on," Char said.

"What are you talking about?" Pearla raised her eyebrows, "Are you messing around? Is there a resident ghost or something?"

"That's the story, at least when we were girls," Max said, looking at Char.

"Yes. We always tried to communicate with her. Her name is Amelia. The legend is that she died in the ocean, walked in and never came out. At least not alive. Her body was never found, but her spirit stayed behind. Her parents were the original owners of the property and the main house before it was modernized and enlarged."

"Are you serious right now?" Pearla looked incredulous. "Because if you are, this is a revenue stream we could tap into. I mean, people love ghost hunting. We're gonna need to re-brand. Snowy Plover Inn: Your destination for relaxation, bird watching, and ghost hunting! How's that sound?"

"I can get behind that," Max agreed.

Chapter 15

Maxine

Having Charlene, Pearla and Krista over for breakfast was just what Maxine needed. They finished up the omelets and made plans for the day. Pearla would interview and hopefully hire some part-time staff to help with cleaning the rooms. There was also a yoga instructor who was looking to rent out the pavilion a few times a week. Max thought it was a good idea as an extra means of revenue, plus the guests were welcome to join in the scheduled classes. Things were getting off to a good start except for the accident, but Max was trying her best to push that thought out of her mind, while also praying for Rose's quick recovery.

She had seen little of Ms. Singer. The author was quiet;

she kept to herself and Max did not want to appear overly solicitous or nosy. At some point she wanted to ask Ms. Singer if she'd consider The Snowy Plover for a writer's retreat, or at least pick the writer's brain on how she might tap into that market. Max was hoping for a time when she could naturally weave that brilliant idea into conversation, maybe this afternoon at the wine and cheese reception, which would presumably be more mellow than yesterday's.

Ms. Singer was booked for the week and not due to check out until Saturday, as were the McMartins, Roxanne and Krista. Professor Lombard was due to leave Friday. So far, no one had canceled the remainder of their stay, and fingers crossed, they wouldn't. Max thought maybe Mr. McMartin might want to leave and re-book accommodations closer to the hospital in Brookhaven, but he hadn't mentioned it. She supposed he would spend the day at the hospital. *At least appear to be concerned about your wife.*

After breakfast, as she and Pearla cleared the dishes and food from the living room, Max took the opportunity to speak with Keith Lombard who was sitting at a sunlit table enjoying his coffee.

"I don't know if I properly thanked you for the nature walk yesterday. It was amazing. Brought back so many childhood memories of coming here. I'm thrilled to get to really learn about all the bird species that call this area home," she said.

"It was my pleasure. I'll be going out today as well. I'm taking a count of each species I see, collecting data. I'd like to bring some students out with me next time, maybe make it an optional research assignment." *So, he's planning on a next time. This is good.*

"What a great idea. I'd love to host your students. Just let me know, and we can make it happen."

"I'll do that," Keith said. He stood to leave, but paused and asked, "Hey, any word on the injured lady? How is she recovering? Does the sheriff have a suspect? Does he think it was foul play?"

Here we go. Max held a neutral expression. *Why is he asking this?*

"I haven't heard anything, other than it was a terrible accident. I'm sure Mrs. McMartin will be just fine."

"Oh, okay," Keith Lombard said and walked through the double doors to the patio courtyard without another word.

Max turned to Pearla.

"That was going so well. Why did he have to bring up the accident? And it WAS an accident!" Pearla said. She was loading the dishes into a plastic bin to take back to the kitchen.

"I know, I just hate all the rumors and the fact that it's all over town being blown way out of proportion. This can't be good publicity for our opening week," Max said.

"Well, as they say, any publicity is good publicity. Besides, everyone is sure to forget it and move on as soon as the next exciting thing happens. Are you still planning on driving to Brookhaven today?"

"Yes, I need to pick up and pay for the rest of the new linens and the small bedside lamps we chose. They're in stock at Home Place. I'm excited to see what they look like in person. It's so hard to tell when you order online. Plus, I'm going to check on Mrs. McMartin. It's the least I can do."

"I'll stay here and man the fort," Pearla said. "I have

those interviews today. I'll text you and let you know how it goes."

"Go team!" Max said with a laugh. "I think Char and Krista are going to explore the village, check out the shops, then kick it by the pool or go walk on the beach. Krista's a great girl. I'm so happy she and Char connected."

"I really like her too," Pearla responded. "I don't care for her boyfriend though, even if I've never met him. Reminds me of the men I date. Unreliable. She deserves better."

Max felt the same. Krista had tried her best to paint Parker in a favorable light, but Max, Char, and Pearla all didn't appreciate that he promised to show up and hadn't. It felt natural to be protective of Krista, even though they barely knew her. Krista deserved better than someone who would string her along and stand her up.

After Max and Pearla loaded the dishwasher, and tidied up the kitchen, Max walked back through the living room and outside to the patio where she saw Ms. Singer seated at one of the small cafe tables. A large umbrella provided shade and her head was bent low as she typed manically on her laptop.

"Have a good day, Ms. Singer," Max called as she passed. Ms. Singer looked up with raised eyebrows and a quick nod, then quickly resumed the frantic typing. She was curious, not a very social person, but maybe authors were that way. Max didn't know any personally, so she had no one to compare her to. She would just grab her purse from the cottage, check in with Char, and be on her way. They would meet up later in the afternoon.

"Hey, Max." Max looked up to see Char and Krista standing on the widow's walk overlooking the inner courtyard. "Come up," Char called. "You need to see something." Max gave a thumbs-up and took the spiral exterior stairs to join them. From the widow's walk you could see all around the property. It encircled the tower which resembled a lighthouse in its design, with a tiny sitting room at the top. As girls, Max and Char often spent time pitching sunflower seeds over the railings at unsuspecting guests and blaming the ghost or sneaking up late at night in their pajamas to look at the stars from the glassed-in room and dream about the future.

"Let's sit in here," Char said, and they gathered in the small enclosed glass room and sat close together on the wrap-around bench seat. "Krista found out some interesting information about Ms. Singer."

"Really?" Max asked. "What did you learn?" Krista had her laptop open, and she sat between Max and Char so they could all view the screen. The only thing showing was the author's official page with a very flattering photo that barely resembled the actual woman. Ms. Singer was not unattractive, but her broad shoulders, height, and short haircut were not obviously feminine. Her online persona was a sharp contrast.

"Well, first off, her name is Melody Singer. Her parents were professional singers, so they thought it'd be cute. I guess she didn't agree."

"Can't blame her for that," Char said.

"It was in an old interview that a fan posted on her blog. I'm sure she doesn't want it publicized."

"But that's not all," Krista continued. "I did a sort of deep dive and found out she's got some skeletons in the closet. She has a carefully curated persona for her fans, but keeps her private life quite private."

"Go on," Max encouraged. "Let's hear it. I love some good gossip."

"She was married twice and both times her spouse died, under 'suspicious circumstances,' but there was never enough evidence to charge her or anyone else with a crime," Krista said.

"Tell Max how they died," Char said.

"The first one fell down two flights of stairs. The second one was hit on the head with some boxes full of books which fell off a shelf in the garage," Krista said.

The three women sat silently for a minute. Max was thinking how ridiculous the notion was that Ms. Singer, a famous author, could be responsible for Rose McMartin's accident.

"Remember when I told you she was a method writer? Which means she fully gets into her characters? I was wondering what that entailed exactly since she's a writer of erotic romance," Char said.

"So you think she tried to injure another guest as research?" Max asked.

"She said she was switching genres. She's currently working on a crime novel, right?" Char said.

"I'd love to peek at the plot outline of her work-in-progress to see if it features an older lady getting offed by her husband's girlfriend," Krista said. Then added, "Oh my gosh, I'm sorry. That was very insensitive."

"But also kind of funny, in a sick sort of way," Char added. "Plus, it's only a thought. And it's what we're all thinking; you just said it out loud."

"Stop, you guys. Enough with the conspiracy theories. I'd like to get through my first week with all my guests leaving while still alive so they can spread the word about this lovely gem of an inn," Max said. It was getting hot in the little enclosed room and she needed some air. She stepped back out to the widow's walk and started down the stairs.

"Enjoy the village, you two. I'll see you later. And maybe leave the investigation and sleuthing to the cop."

"Alright, alright, we'll see you later," Char said.

Max gathered her purse, and her insulated water bottle from her cottage for the trip to Brookhaven. She'd had navy-blue stainless steel water bottles made with the inn's signature Snowy Plover logo and they'd turned out great. They were available for purchase in the reception area along with other gifts she'd designed, t-shirts and dish towels, magnets, and postcards suitable for framing.

On the drive to Brookhaven, her phone rang and transferred to her car's speaker system. Sawyer. With the sound of his voice, Max felt a surge of motherly love and emotion. They'd last spoken on Friday, and in her rush to set up the hotel and in the confusion of all that happened since, Max hadn't thought to text or call him. *I can't believe I forgot to call him.*

"Mom, are you okay? I haven't heard from you." There was concern in his voice.

"I'm fine, honey. Sorry for not calling. Opening the inn has been overwhelming and by the time I remembered to call, it was late and I didn't want to trouble you. How's school? Classes good?"

"Never mind that, Mom. Yes, it's all fine with me. Trouble me with what? Is there something I should know?" She could picture him perfectly, his tousled too-long hair, his face with a troubled look.

Max gave Sawyer the briefest version of the events.

She didn't want to worry him and assured him Char was there, no need for him to cut classes and drive for hours. Nothing to be concerned about. He told her about his courses and his roommates and how he may have an internship possibility for summer. Max was hoping he'd spend the summer with her, but she would not force it. The main reason, or one reason she'd bought the inn, was to have a life of her own. She didn't want Sawyer to feel obligated to be with her, to worry about her. *He needs to have his own life; I want that for him.*

After picking up the bedside lamps and linens, Max stopped for a coffee. She got a large Americano to go and drove to the visitors' lot of Brookhaven Hospital. This time she went straight to Rose's room, bypassing the nurses' station. Max didn't want to be denied a visit. She looked in the small window first, and seeing no one else in the room, went in. Rose was lying on her back, slightly propped up, covered to her neck, but looking pale and still. Her eyes were closed; blue veins visible on her eyelids. Rose's head was tightly bandaged. Her face was bruised a deep purple. An IV bag with light yellow liquid dripped slowly, and the monitor showed her regularly beating heart. Max leaned in toward her face.

"Rose? Can you hear me? It's Maxine from the inn. I just came to see how you're doing," she whispered. It was impossible to tell if the woman was asleep or still unconscious. Either way, Max knew she didn't have permission to be there.

"I'll leave you now and I hope you feel better soon," she said and exited the room. At the nurses' station she paused to ask about Rose's condition.

"How is Mrs. McMartin doing? I came to visit her,"

Max said.

"Oh no. No visitors. Not even family right now. We had to give her a strong sedative, she was very confused earlier, very agitated," the nurse replied.

"Why? What happened?"

"What is your name, please?" the nurse asked tersely.

"It's Maxine Egan. I'm the owner of Snowy Plover Inn where the McMartins are staying. The accident happened there. I wanted to check on Mrs. McMartin. I'm concerned about her." The nurse's expression softened and she leaned in.

"Well, she regained consciousness when her husband was here and she started yelling and getting very worked up. She accused him of cheating on her. Then she said his girlfriend, Roxanne, tried to kill her. She tried to get up, and we had to restrain her. The doctor gave her a sedative to calm her down."

"Whoa. That's intense," Max said. *Is it though?*

"Her husband got very upset and left. He said Roxanne is a friend of Rose's and not his girlfriend. I tried to explain that it's common for people with head injuries to talk nonsense, and that he shouldn't get offended. I'm sure she didn't mean it, but he said to call him when she calms down. He was shaken up."

"Is he still here, at the hospital?"

"I don't think so. He said he was going to call their daughter, then go back to the inn in Silvermist."

"Was there another lady with him?" Max asked.

"No. That's why I asked your name. I wondered if you were the friend, Roxanne," the nurse said. Max knew the nurse was telling her more than she should. *It's not my place to remind her of privacy protocols.*

"May I leave you with my number?"

Max rummaged through her purse and pulled out a Snowy Plover Inn business card, then scribbled her personal cell number on the back and slid it across the counter.

"When Rose feels up to it, please let her know she can call me. When do you think she'll be released?"

"She'll probably stay a couple more days for observation. It's a pretty significant head injury. Swelling from concussions can take a while to subside."

"Thanks for filling me in. I'll call tomorrow to check if she can have visitors before driving over. I appreciate you explaining her condition. I hope she heals soon."

Max sat in her car sipping her now cold coffee. She almost wished the nurse hadn't over-shared. It was none of her business and now she had information that she wasn't sure what to do with. Was she obligated to tell the sheriff? Should she call him and suggest he take a statement from the nurse who heard Rose accuse Roxanne of trying to kill her? Or was it the rantings of a woman with a concussion whose husband might be cheating on her, but also might not? What to do? She would discuss it with Pearla when she got back and then decide. Rose was safe in her hospital bed and Walt and Roxanne were both at the inn, as far as she knew.

Chapter 16

Pearla

Pearla asked herself if she'd forgotten anything. So far the list read: refresh rooms every two days if requested, laundry, vacuum and dust living room, sweep and steam hard floors, sweep hallways, inventory food, replenish items in the gift store display, answer calls, return calls, take online reservations, advertise, purchase food and wine for breakfast and reception. List-making centered her. Instead of feeling overwhelmed, she felt empowered. She was new to the profession of running an inn, but she was a quick study and a fast worker. Plus, she considered organization as her super power. So, Maxine had tasked her with interviewing potential employees for part time help. Since arriving three weeks ago and moving into the studio apartment above reception, she along with Max, had been listing daily duties to determine what they could do themselves and when and where they would need an extra set of hands.

"I think we start with one or two part-time employees and reassess as needed," Max said.

"I agree," Pearla said.

"Mr. Trawl and his son are taking care of the grounds and basic maintenance, and everything we've asked them to do, they have, so I think we're good there for now," Max said.

"I asked to see a schedule of gardening and pool care, and I didn't get the best reaction. The son gives me the creeps. I feel like he's always around, but I don't see him ever actually doing anything," Pearla responded.

"Let's not rock the boat yet. We'll keep an eye out, and as long as the work is getting done, we'll let them be. I've been leaving a to-do list for them in the shed. Neither one is particularly talkative, or friendly."

The inn got little outside foot traffic. People would sometimes pass through on their way to the shore using the trail at the back of the property which connected with the public trail. A call button at the front desk alerted Pearla or Max, whomever was signed in, if someone was waiting there and needed assistance. They'd displayed the gift items in a glass-fronted, locked hutch. A price list hung framed on the wall next to it. Surplus items were stored in the cellar. With these features in place, it wasn't strictly necessary that someone be stationed at all times at the reception desk. The previous owners used this system, so they kept it.

One thing Max and Pearla had changed was the

antiquated reservation system. The inn had a website, but the site had no functionality. Interested guests couldn't check room rates or availability online. It was basically an advertisement with photos and a phone number. You had to call and speak to someone to reserve a room or, more often than not, leave a message and wait for a return call. It was old-school and suited the usual patrons who appreciated simplicity. Most of the regulars were accustomed to making future reservations before they checked out from their current stay. Staff hand wrote the reservations in a date book kept in the office. Through the years, these loyal guests and word of mouth had been all that sustained the little inn. Both Pearla and Max believed there was potential for so much more, maybe even an expansion in a few years.

Pearla scheduled three interviews, thirty minutes apart. Emma, her first interviewee, was younger, in her twenties, and reminded Pearla of a typical high school student from Royal. She chewed a large wad of neon green gum, and her copper braid hung down to her waist. After a few minutes, she froze mid-sentence, mid-chew, and apologized for the gum and asked for a tissue to spit it out.

"I'm so sorry. I quit smoking but find I need a distraction. I'm mortified I forgot to spit it out. I'd never chew it around the guests, I promise," she said. Pearla chuckled, deciding she could forget about the gum. Emma had cleaned houses with her mom and was taking classes online in accounting, and Pearla respected that she apologized for the gum.

After the interviews, Pearla's inclination was to hire all three immediately, but after each candidate's interview wrapped-up she said, "Let me get back to you in the next couple days after I discuss it with the owner. It was a pleasure meeting you."

Both of the ladies, Emma and Sylvie, wanted ten to fifteen hours a week and had flexible schedules. Charles was looking for some hours on the weekends.

"I'm very handy, a quick learner, and willing to do any type of job you need," he'd said. Pearla liked the idea of a third employee knowing the ins-and-outs of the grounds maintenance, though she wasn't sure how the Trawls might feel about it, or how open they'd be to training someone. *Well, too bad. It's not your call.* Sylvie cleaned vacation rentals on an as-needed basis and was looking for some permanent hours each week.

Pearla phoned Max to relay the news of three prospective employees and to tell her she'd found a locksmith with availability to come today. She only received her voicemail.

"Max, it's me. Lots of good news. Just call back when you get a chance." She thought of following up with a text, but didn't. Sitting at her desk, she pulled up the newly updated Snowy Plover Inn website. It showed two new reservations for the next month. The yoga instructor had canceled and rebooked her appointment to look at the pavilion, and it was just as well. Pearla's stomach was protesting, letting her know she'd forgotten to eat lunch.

She walked through the pool area and gathered some used towels. The inn was equipped with three industrial washers and dryers that could handle all the laundry. They changed linens and towels in the rooms every other day unless requested by guests. Guests could ring the front desk or leave a message if they needed extras. Pool and beach towels were in two wicker chests between the pool and hot tub. They'd put a supply of sweat towels in the pavilion for guests who wanted to use it for yoga or a floor workout. Max and Pearla had discussed adding a second pavilion with gym equipment, but wondered if it would spoil the rustic vibe of the inn. Did people come here to work out on gym equipment, or to leave it behind for a few days?

Pearla was finishing a peanut butter and jelly sandwich and a cold lemon water when she heard a car pull up. She peeked out one of her front windows and saw a blue van with a large font declaring, "Brookhaven Lock & Key." When a man stepped out of the vehicle, she called down, "I'll be right with you." Pearla's tense shoulders relaxed, and leaving the crusts of her sandwich, she headed downstairs.

She'd called the locksmith early this morning and left a message explaining it was urgent she get an appointment for today. The encounter with Colby Trawl the previous night had her concerned about who had keys to what. She bet the old owners didn't keep track well. The keys to the rooms were the old-fashioned type, large, brass, and heavy, but nostalgic. She and Max agreed that the long-time visitors would balk if all the locks were changed over to electronic ones. They were too modern and the wrong aesthetic. Each room was equipped with a slider security lock which one could engage once in their room. For now, those old-style locks would remain. There were other more pressing issues to consider before changing out all the guest room locks.

Pearla was most concerned with the private residences of herself and Max; these were the locks to be changed today. She supposed that the Trawls having access to the inn's main master lock made sense as they were in charge of maintenance. However, they would need to check in with her or Max and sign out for the master key as needed. The procedure would be the same for the keys to the cellar and storage areas, as well as the front office. It wasn't enough to have the doors marked Private. No guest should have been able to wander downstairs. The common halls, the foyer with reception area, the living room/lounge would stay open to guests. The outside restrooms, pool changing area, and yoga studio would remain available. Guests could access these as well as exterior entrance doors with a credit card style electronic key, or by punching in a key code.

They weren't sure yet about how to secure the kitchen. It connected with the front reception, walk-in pantry, and living room through convenient swinging doors. *Who'd have thought we'd need to, but here we are.*

Once they were trained on the use of the security cameras, that should suffice. They would be alerted if anyone entered the kitchen and the door would stay marked: Private. So many things to think of, but all of this was new territory for them, a new venture. Instead of regret, Pearla felt excitement. It was thrilling to be here.

A rumpled man in gray coveralls came up the steps and met her in the reception foyer. His hair had a precise side-part and was combed through with shiny pomade. He greeted Pearla with a warm smile, showing tobacco-stained teeth.

"Hi there. Name's Nate from the Lock and Key. My boss says you need a couple locks re-keyed." Pearla shook Nate's outstretched hand. It felt rough, and she noticed scabs on the knuckles.

"Nice to meet you, Nate. I'm Pearla Beckett, the general manager. Thanks for making it out here today. If you'll just follow me, I can point out the locks we need changed." She led him through the foyer and into the living room. They took the stairs to the left, and at the top of the landing, arrived at her studio apartment. An open hall with a railing led to the other guest rooms on this floor. There were two smaller rooms, each with queen beds. These small rooms shared a bathroom conveniently located between them. Guests needed to exit their room to access it, but as such, these older rooms were priced lower. At the opposite end of the hall above the kitchen was the deluxe suite where Krista was staying. Pearla felt it was the nicest room of the inn with the best views second only to her studio apartment.

"Is this the only door to your apartment?" Nate asked.

"No, there's a second entry outside that's on the way up to the widow's walk," Pearla said.

"I didn't realize people in California knew that term. I'm from the east coast and that's a common feature on the coastal houses. I always pictured ghostly ladies pacing the widow walks in the evening fog, waiting for their husbands' whaling boats to come in."

"From ours, you can see a sliver of the ocean. Can't see boats unless you've got binoculars though. Still, I love walking around up there. It's a great vantage point, almost like a bird's-eye view. Since there's very little light pollution, the stars are amazing." Since she'd moved to the Snowy Plover, not a day passed that Pearla didn't go out to the widow's walk for fresh air or to enjoy the enchanting view. She still felt like she had to pinch herself to make sure she really lived here.

Nate had the doorknob and deadbolt off in a matter of seconds. He set the pieces in his canvas shoulder bag. Then Pearla walked him through the apartment to the back entry and second lock.

"What a great place you have here. These high ceilings are spectacular. Good light for painting, too."

"Thanks, I quite like it myself," Pearla said. "Can you key these locks the same, please?"

"Yes. Will do," Nate said as he deftly removed the second door knob and deadbolt, then added those to his canvas bag. "I'll re-key these with the mobile machine in the van. How many sets of keys do you want?"

Pearla thought a moment before responding, "Three, please." She figured Max should have one, she should have one, and a spare they could lock in the wall safe. For Max's cottage, she'd request four, enough for personal guests and when Sawyer came to stay. On the way to the cottage, she passed Colby Trawl, and to be friendly, she said, "What are you up to today, Mr. Trawl?"

He looked around as if she might be addressing someone other than him, then replied, "Maintenance. Fixing a lightbulb," and kept walking past. As with every encounter she had with the Trawls, Pearla felt slight unease. She led Nate to Maxine's cottage, where he quickly removed the front and back door locks. Pearla wished there was someone to stay and monitor Max's cottage.

"I'll get these changed out and I'll meet you back at reception. Then you can try all the keys. That should be it. I'll need about forty-five minutes to finish," Nate said.

Pearla wanted to check on her apartment and also wanted to keep tabs on Colby Trawl. She took the circular stairs to the widow's walk and stopped in her tracks when Colby Trawl nearly bumped into her on his way down. *My apartment's unlocked.*

"What were you doing up there?" she asked more

forcefully than she would have liked.

"Changing a lightbulb in the tower room," he replied, and pushed past her. It was too close for comfort as he brushed up against her.

"Wait," Pearla said.

"What?" he asked impatiently. *What the hell were you doing near my apartment? Did you go in?*

"Thank you," Pearla responded, trying to keep her voice level. Colby Trawl looked at her, then turned and walked away. Pearla wanted to check her apartment to see if anything was disturbed, a different thought overcame her, and instead she ran after Colby. She caught up to him and the words rushed out with no time to plan.

"Hey, I forgot to ask you something last night when you came into the cellar."

"Yeah? What?" The agitation steamed off him. *Boy, this guy's a charmer.*

"Why did you come to the cellar in the first place? Did you know there was a mess to clean up?" Pearla studied his face for a reaction. *Did his left eye just twitch?*

He paused. Was it Pearla's imagination or was he crafting a response? Was he sharp enough to do that? Could she catch him in a lie?

"No. I was just there to finish moving and unloading the delivery boxes, and to lock up."

"Oh, okay. Thanks," Pearla said and left it at that. *Last night he said he heard about a mess to clean and he mentioned bleach to get the blood smell out. How would he know that?* She wondered if she should contact the sheriff, but what would she say? If Sheriff Silva wasn't concerned, neither should she be. *I've always had an overactive imagination.*

Chapter 17

Sheriff Silva

Sheriff Rene Silva sat in his rolling office chair in the small space he shared with Janice, the postmaster. Only a flimsy door separated them, and most of the time he left it ajar to avoid claustrophobia. His office lacked a window. He was watching the clock and thinking about the steak he'd left marinating at home. He had access to an actual office in Brookhaven, but when hired for his current post in Silvermist Point, he insisted he be provided an adequate office space in town so as not to have to drive back and forth for data entry. Most days he stayed in Silvermist and, at the end of his shift, retreated to his little cabin outfitted with Wi-Fi and kept to himself. He wasn't one for a thriving social life. Earl, his gray cat, was good enough company.

He was thinking about leaving for the day when the call came through.

"Hi Sheriff," there was hesitation in the woman's voice, "this is Beth. I work at Miscellaneous Goods."

"Yes, Beth. How can I help you?"

"I have a concern I wanted to bring to your attention. I was working my shift when a person I didn't recognize came in. Well…", and here there was an awkward pause, "they were flirting with me." Rene Silva laughed inwardly. Beth was an older woman, a much older woman, and not a cougar. He was positive no one was flirting with her.

"I'm sorry someone was bothering you, but unless it was extreme, or sexual harassment, it's just a nuisance, not a crime," he said gently.

"Oh, I know. It's not only the flirting that concerns me, it's the questions that were asked," Beth said. Sheriff Silva took the pen he had tucked behind his ear and flipped his yellow legal pad to a fresh page, ready to take notes if needed.

"It made me uncomfortable, the flirting, because I'm not that sort. I'm a Christian woman, after all."

Sheriff Silva rolled his eyes, and waited, as he heard Beth take in a dramatic breath.

"This person started off just making conversation. You know, asking about the size of the town, whether I knew our crime rates, and what size police force we have. Lots of questions, and all the time staring at me. When this stranger asked about a place to stay, I mentioned The Snowy Plover. Then they said how terrible it was to hear someone had died there."

"Died?" the sheriff asked.

"Yes. They went on to say they heard a lady was murdered there yesterday. And I told them they were mistaken. No one died, and most definitely, no one was murdered. There was only an older lady who had fallen. I know this town is small, Sheriff, but gee whiz, it surprised me a stranger would know anything about it. And it got me wondering, how *would* a stranger know?"

"I agree that's peculiar. You say you've never seen this person before? Did you ask what brought them to town?"

"No, it didn't occur to me to ask."

"Did you get a name? Did the person pay by credit card?"

"No. Cash. And I didn't ask for a name, sorry."

"Description?"

"Hard to say, really. You'll see what I mean. Since I thought the whole thing was weird, I snapped a couple photos on my phone. I don't think they noticed. I was discreet."

"Was anyone else in the store at the time?"

"No, it's just me working today. Nick called in sick and the owners are on vacation, gone through the weekend. I don't remember if there were other customers at the time. I'm about to close up."

Rene Silva could hear the bells ring from the front door of the shop.

"Oh, hold on. I have a customer. Can you just stop by tomorrow morning? I've got the first shift. I can show you the photos then. Say nine-thirty?" Rene could tell Beth was keen to hang up.

"Yes, I'll see you at nine-thirty. We can talk more then."

Rene hung up and stretched his back in his substandard office chair, glad to get her off the phone. *She'll have calmed down by tomorrow.* He had been finally getting used to low, or no drama in his post as sheriff of Silvermist Point. At first, he'd missed his time with the LAPD and the ever-present action, but now his days were predictable and most nights he was free to relax off the clock, knowing the night shift calls, if there were any, would be routed to Brookhaven. It had been years since he'd worked a normal day shift with only the occasional call to assist with a nighttime emergency and he was enjoying the schedule and the work pace.

Currently, there were no open cases in Silvermist, no crimes to solve. Sure, there were neighborly disputes: cars parked on someone else's property, petty theft by teens, a couple of fistfights to break up at the bar, things like that. Nothing serious in the nine months since he'd taken the job. Rene knew he'd bungled the investigation at Snowy Plover yesterday. *Was it really necessary to follow protocol?* He'd taken photos and interviewed guests, but that was all. He'd not called in to request a forensics person and he'd agreed to let the staff at the inn clean up the mess, effectively destroying evidence. The lady wasn't dead so, no harm, no foul, and after completing his interviews, he was confident that even if someone had intended to kill Rose McMartin, they'd been unsuccessful. The woman was alive, recovering in the hospital, and would live.

But now it appeared there might be a case to solve, someone was asking questions, and he wasn't excited about it. He was getting too used to being complacent and comfortable. *Am I going soft? Losing my edge?* He went home and grilled his steak. He ate it with a baked potato and salad and a delicate glass of Merlot, falling asleep on his lumpy sofa in front of the TV with Earl Gray curled up at his feet.

Chapter 18

Charlene

Charlene grabbed a towel from the wicker chest and spread it on one of the lounge chairs between the pool and hot tub. She wore a thick terry-cloth robe and planned to read for a while, swim a few laps, then relax in the hot tub. The outdoor solar lights and full moon weren't quite bright enough to read by and she was glad she thought to bring her clip-on book light. Disappointment hovered, but she knew she couldn't go with the others down to the shore. It was the right decision. She sensed a flare-up coming on with her arthritis, and if she pushed herself too hard, she'd be debilitated tomorrow and would need time to recover. The night was beautiful and clear with a bright full moon and no wind, a rarity for this part of the coast which usually featured fog, wind, darkness, or all three.

Max had thoughtfully suggested they take the all-terrain golf cart, so Char could come too, but when she went to retrieve it, it wasn't parked in the usual place behind the shed.

"Sorry, Char. We don't have to go. We'll stay here and do something else. We can play cards." But Char wouldn't hear of it. They'd made the plans that afternoon and Professor Lombard was eager to join them. Charlene would not spoil it for them.

"Absolutely not! You all go on. I'm perfectly happy to read my book. I packed a steamy romance that I'm dying to start. It's by Ms. Singer. I'm hoping she'll sign it for me." She settled in and Butters sidled up to her chair, staring with expectant eyes.

"Come on up, Butters." Char patted her lap. "I'll give you some attention."

She and Max had walked to the shore in the moonlight many times as girls. They would bring flashlights, but kept them switched off, relying on their eyes adjusting to the darkness. Each time they hoped to encounter the ghost of Amelia. Sometimes on an otherwise still night, a slight breeze would blow. They would whisper, "Hello, Amelia. We come in peace. Show yourself." Once they imagined they saw Amelia's nightgown floating in the water, but as they got closer to the shore break, they admitted it was only kelp.

Charlene was immersed in chapter five, with Butters snuggled in and purring like a little motor, when a splashing noise caught her attention. Larry Trawl was next to the pool using a skimmer to fetch out leaves. Butters jumped down to investigate. *Isn't it late to be doing this?*

"Good evening," Char said, setting her book in her lap.

"Evening," Larry Trawl said and continued long sweeps across the surface of the still water.

"You probably don't remember me, but Maxine and I used to come here quite often as kids. It's been a long time since I've visited. It's still as I remember though."

"I remember you," he said, then walked around the edge of the pool and came to stand close to her lounge chair.

"You and your friend were a couple of pains in the …" Larry interrupted himself with a gruff laugh. *Was it a laugh, or is he serious?*

"I'm not sure what you mean," Char said with a nervous giggle to lighten the mood. *What was he talking about?*

"You used to like to get my son in trouble, if I remember correctly. All he wanted was to be your friend." *Your son was a weirdo, and still is.*

"Oh. I'm afraid I can't recall any of that." Char pulled her robe tighter around her. "But I'll offer a belated apology for anything rude my teenage self may have done. No hard feelings," Char said, forcing a lighthearted laugh, then picked up her book to subtly message that she was done with the conversation.

"Sure. You have a pleasant night then," Larry Trawl said as he skimmed the pool to gather the last of the stray leaves, before disappearing into the darkness.

At chapter seven, Char set her book down, took off her robe and walked into the pool. The sloped entrance and pebble bottom felt like a swimming hole in the woods, but the clean salt water and perfect, just-right temperature were more like a luxury spa. Always cool enough to be refreshing on a hot day, yet still warm enough not to give you the chills if you wanted a night swim. Char needed to remember to take photos. This was the exact pool she wanted in her dream house she had yet to build in a location, as yet, unchosen.

Being near weightless in the salt water was just what she needed for her achy joints and she swam laps across the widest area of the pool. At first, she doggy-paddled to avoid wetting her hair, but eventually she dunked under and let the water caress her in full relaxation. How many hours had she and Max spent here? She was twelve again, as fond childhood memories enveloped her; she marveled at how time flies by in an instant and how important it is to savor each moment.

Done with her swim, Charlene got out and walked the short distance, dripping, to the ten-person hot tub. She pressed the button to activate the bubbles and eased into the warmth, sighing. She sat with her arms folded behind her neck, eyes closed, resting and relaxing until she was startled and opened her eyes.

"Mind if I join you?" Roxanne asked, though regardless of the answer, she was already lowering herself into the bubbles and steam.

"Of course not," Char said. "How are you holding up? You must be so worried about your friend."

"I am," Roxanne said. "It was such an unfortunate accident," she paused for a sip of wine from a plastic stemless glass. "Poor Walt."

"Yes, I can imagine how worried he must be about his wife. Any word on how Rose is feeling?" *You know, the one who was actually injured?*

"Walt went to see her today. He's not back yet. He must still be in Brookhaven. I've just been here alone all day and night. I walked to the village for lunch and ate the leftovers for dinner. This was supposed to be a fun getaway," she lamented. "I hope he's back soon."

Could you be more dramatic?

Char wasn't sure what to make of this woman, or the whole situation with Rose's injury. Max had relayed earlier what she found out at the hospital and Pearla had shared her suspicion about Colby Trawl. Charlene wondered if they all were being overly paranoid. The Trawls were strange men and Roxanne clearly had a crush on Walt, but would either try to injure or murder Rose McMartin? Would an author attempt to kill a random woman for research? None of it made sense. The only explanation that felt plausible was an unfortunate freak accident.

Chapter 19

Tuesday
Krista

A ping on her phone awoke Krista. *Why did I plug it in across the room?* The only reason she got out of bed was to check if it was Char. They were planning a visit to the village again. Her bed here was so luxurious and comfortable, and she'd slept so deeply once again, she had no clue of the time. It wasn't Char. It was Parker with another empty promise that he would definitely arrive today. At this point, Krista wasn't sure she wanted him to. She was having fun on her own and enjoying the company of other women who felt like friends. She did not want anyone to interfere with the building of her first close female relationships.

Krista typed: Parker, it's fine if you can't make it. I understand. I'm enjoying myself and staying busy. The town is charming and I'm realizing just how much I needed a break from work. *And you.* I'll see you when I get home.

Her finger hovered over the Send button. And then she backspaced and deleted the entire message, opting for a simple: Great, see you then! She added a smiley face and hit Send. No point in asking what time. *He's playing games, but I won't play.*

She rolled back over and slept some more. *It's my vacation after all.*

Chapter 20

Charlene

Char was grateful Max had offered to drive them to the village. The gentle yoga she'd practiced this morning had lessened her pain, but the damp air didn't help. The distance was short, and she'd walked it many times in her youth, but she felt her joints stiffening and knew to not disobey the warning. As the ladies approached Books and Brew, they noticed several others gathered out front. Tom opened the glass front door, and the hanging bell clanged as the small gathering stepped in, greeted by Tom's warm smile and hearty, "Hello," along with the enticing scent of rich, dark roast coffee.

"Hi, Tom," Max said as she passed.

"Hi, Max," he said back, smiling.

"Morning," Andrew called from across the store. "You all are my first patrons of the day."

The shop held copies of new and used books, along with a changing display of touristy trinkets. The new titles were more or less in order by genre and author, with featured copies on a round table at the front. Local authors had their own dedicated shelf, also positioned at the front. The older, previously owned copies were supposed to be organized, but it wasn't uncommon to find a thriller in sci-fi or a rom-com shoved into the classics. The hunt was always satisfying. Max and Pearla wanted coffees and headed to the back counter.

Run by the current owners, Andrew and Tom, Books and Brew was a warm and inviting space. They had recently built up a following from their book discussion podcast, also called Books and Brew, where during each episode they mentioned the bookstore and reminded listeners, "If you're ever in Silvermist Point, do stop by and say hello." Char figured the podcast had contributed to the increased foot traffic. *Good for them. The world needs bookstores.*

Silvermist Point was often driven past by travelers on their way to somewhere else, and considered a sleepy little enclave with not much to offer. However, as girls Char and Max had kept themselves plenty entertained. For those looking to escape the hustle of their regular lives, and who wanted a sort of forced slowdown, Silvermist Point with its quaint little village and eerie, sometimes desolate, windswept coast, was just right. Once again Char wondered why she'd stayed away so long. Krista interrupted her thoughts.

"Someone, make me stop," Krista said as she carried a stack of books with a puzzle balanced on top to the register. Andrew looked delighted.

"Nice selection. You've got eclectic taste. Are you familiar with our podcast?" he asked while handing her a bookmark with the information. "I think you'll like it." Krista agreed and said it sounded right up her alley. She bought two linen shopping bags with the Books and Brews logo to carry her purchases.

Charlene chose two titles she hadn't read, then she and Krista joined Pearla and Max who were enjoying a coffee with Tom. Max introduced them.

"I love your shop," Char said. "We missed you yesterday when we were in town. You had the 'Back Soon' sign up."

"Well, I'm glad you made it today," Tom said.

"What a dream," Krista said. "Imagine spending your day with shelves of adventures just waiting to be discovered. I'm jealous. You guys have the perfect job."

"We're fond of it, and always happy to meet other bibliophiles," he said grinning widely.

Max and Pearla finished their coffees then led the way to Miscellaneous Goods.

"I just need to grab a few things for this afternoon's reception," Pearla said. "But, I think you'll want to check out the store. Miscellaneous Goods is a unique space. I always find things I didn't know I needed. It can be dangerous. You've been warned."

Miscellaneous Goods was just a few doors down. Max offered to take Char and Krista's bags and put them in the trunk. She had thoughtfully parked directly in front of Books and Brew. Char appreciated the offer and Max's sensitivity. She was using her cane to steady her balance, and it was challenging to carry bags. When they arrived at the storefront, they were surprised to find it dark with the sign in the glass door front turned to *Closed*. The hours posted were nine to seven.

"Huh," Char mumbled, "that's weird." She checked her phone. It was 9:43.

Pearla put her hands to the glass front door and tried to peer inside. It was loose, unlocked, and she easily pushed it in.

"Maybe they forgot to lock-up when they closed," she said, and called out through the crack in the door, "Hey, is anyone here?"

Char's skin prickled. Something felt off, but she said, "Let's go in and at least see if we can lock it, or contact the owners. Tom and Andrew must have their number."

Pearla was first to step inside, followed by Char who sniffed as she entered. It smelled like pickles and wine and something else. The store was dim with the only light source from the glass front. Once inside, the movement of the women set off the automatic lights which took their eyes a second to adjust to.

"Holy crap!" Char blurted as she noticed several shelves knocked over and glass jars broken on the tile floor.

"It looks like there was a fight in here," Pearla said.

"Or an earthquake," Max said.

"Maybe they were robbed. We should check the register," Krista suggested while stepping gingerly through the mess.

"This is wine. And I see some pickle jars, sauces and spices, but this," Char said pointing, "looks like blood."

"Probably ketchup," Max said.

"No, pretty sure it's blood," Pearla said. "And the way it's smeared…" She hesitated before adding, "Someone was hurt here, and dragged."

All four sets of eyes followed the smear across the tile floor to where it abruptly ended.

"Where's the body?" Pearla was thinking aloud and spoke the question at the front of everyone's mind. Charlene felt her stomach turn and wanted to sit down as her nose recognized and was overcome with the iron tang of blood over the wine and pickle smell. Krista went behind the counter and pressed the open button on the old-style register. The drawer flung out.

"I don't think they were robbed," she reported. "The register is full of cash and receipts."

Max joined her behind the counter, "The phone's off the hook."

Pearla was in the back of the store and shouted, "The backdoor isn't locked. Or the security screen. I'm gonna check the isles and make sure there's not a …"

"Body," Char said shakily. She had found a chair and was now sitting, trying to catch her breath and not panic. *Keep it together. There's no danger.*

"We need to call the sheriff," Char said, though she actually wanted to leave, to let someone else discover this mess. *Calm down, calm down.*

"I'm on it," Pearla had her phone in hand and was already scrolling for the number. "I put his number in my phone on Sunday. Here it is: Sheriff Rene Silva." Pearla was walking around, checking out the rest of the store while Max and Krista stayed behind the sales counter.

"Yes, Sheriff, this is Pearla Beckett. I'm at Miscellaneous Goods and it looks like there was a robbery," she paused, "and possibly an injury. There's what appears to be blood. And no one's here. The door was unlocked, so we came in to investigate." Charlene and the others watched and waited, as Pearla listened to the sheriff's response.

"Okay, we'll wait here for you." Pearla hung up. "He's on his way. He said he was supposed to come by this morning to speak with Beth, but he got busy and forgot the time. He said we shouldn't touch anything."

In a matter of minutes, Rene Silva arrived, bursting through the door, all official. He started taking notes on a small spiral pad and snapping pictures with his phone. Char wasn't sure what to make of him. His manner was brusque and all business, but the way he pulled at the collar of his uniform and hiked up his pants, made her wonder if he was masking genuine concern, or nerves, or something else.

"You ladies are free to leave. I'll follow up here with an investigation."

"What does that mean?" Char blurted. "Won't you share anything with us? Like theories about what happened here? We're the ones who discovered the scene, right?" She felt her face redden. She hadn't meant to be so demanding, but it was hard to walk away with unanswered questions, though minutes before that's what she'd wanted to do. Max, of course, was more reasonable and said, "Will you please let us know what you find out, Sheriff? We'd appreciate it." The sheriff swept his eyes over each of the women, then he fixed his gaze on Max.

"This is the second accident you've been involved with in just a few days." He paused to let his words stay suspended in the tension. *What's he implying?*

"Your job keeps you busy. Is that what you mean?" Pearla asked, pointedly. Then she suggested, "Talk to Andrew and Tom at Books and Brew. They can get you the owner's number and might be helpful in other ways."

"I'll be in touch, if I need you. It looks like Beth took a spill, then went home for the night and forgot to lock up. Usually the simplest explanation is the actual one," Sheriff Silva said as he ushered them out the door, which he promptly locked behind them, leaving the sign turned to the Closed side.

The ladies stood on the sidewalk, looking around, too stunned to speak. The blinds in the front window flipped shut and the shade was pulled down on the front door, blocking any view from passersby. Charlene was first to speak.

"I say we move up the wine tasting plan. What time does Gracious Grapes open? I could use a drink."

"Sadly, not till two," Pearla responded. "And Barnaby's not till three. But let's go to Front Porch. I should be able to get a few things there for this afternoon's reception, and I'll fill in the rest with stock from the pantry. I don't want to go into Brookhaven today, I have too many other tasks to do."

Chapter 21

Maxine

This is terrible publicity for the inn," Maxine lamented as she read over the newsletter again, hoping the headline would magically change. "I wonder who puts this out?" The four ladies were gathered in Max's sitting room. Each held a glass of chilled chardonnay.

"I bet it's the woman in the post office, Janice. She's right next to the sheriff. Probably privy to any and all that goes on in Silvermist. Which we know isn't a whole lot, especially on the crime front," Pearla said. *Until now.*

"This is just the type of gossip that small town folks love. A mystery to solve. Something to talk about. Fingers to point." Max held the light bluish-gray paper, with "Silvermist Point of View" typed across the front. A pair of glasses and an old-fashioned fountain pen decorated the corners.

"It's so amateur," Krista offered. "I bet no one even reads this thing."

The damning article was short, but it was front and center and practically shouting off the page: **Suspicious Injury at Snowy Plover Inn**.

Sunday evening, time unknown, a guest was mysteriously injured at the newly re-opened Snowy Plover Inn. The victim was an older woman who was bludgeoned with a heavy object. She sustained a serious head injury and was transported to Brookhaven Medical Center by ambulance. Guests were interviewed, but no arrests have been made, and no official comment was given by their staff. Is danger lurking in our little town? Stay tuned.

"Who would write this?" Char asked. "There's no name, just 'Staff Writer.' Ugh! So much easier to hide behind the keyboard."

"Nice part about, *no official comment from staff*," Pearla groaned. "As if we were asked for a comment and refused to give one."

Max read through the rest of the newsletter. It could hardly be called a local paper. It had simple graphics and consisted of three sheets of paper folded and stapled together. Most of it was filler, the same type of content Max had helped her students insert into the school newsletter at Royal High: word search, weather stories, local sales and coupons, and an advice column. At the bottom of the last page was a request to subscribe online for a digital copy. Max wondered what the readership was. Would everyone in town have read it? She would ask Tyne about it next time she saw him. *I'm not calling him and giving this even more attention.*

The ladies had discovered the offending newsletter

earlier at The Front Porch Bakery where several patrons sat in wicker chairs on the actual front porch reading it and side-eyeing them as they entered. A stack was piled in a basket on the counter and had been delivered earlier that morning. The young barista said they received new issues of the "Silvermist Point of View" sporadically. That morning the stack was waiting on the front porch when he arrived at six to open.

"Where else are the newsletters delivered?" Max had asked.

"Oh, everywhere," he said. "All the stores on Main get copies."

"Fantastic," Max said as she spied the headline. "Who do I speak with regarding the accuracy of the reporting?" The kid only looked confused, and he didn't offer an answer.

"Oh, never mind," Max had said. *Don't blame this kid, he has nothing to do with it.* Pearla bought her necessary items and they left immediately; it was not the time to browse. On the short ride back, they theorized who could have written the headline and why.

"Hopefully the excitement will die down quickly. It won't be long before the townsfolk hear about what happened at Miscellaneous Goods. I hope the sheriff finds the missing lady. That's a real news story," Max said.

"Hey, what time does Miscellaneous Goods close? Does anyone know?" Char asked.

"Seven," Pearla said. "Why?"

"Last night I was in the hot tub with Roxanne and she said Walt still wasn't back. That was after eight," Char said.

"So are you thinking he had something to do with Beth's disappearance?" Max asked. "That seems like a stretch."

"But what if Beth was the one who wrote the story? Maybe Walt was mad at her for calling out the accident for what it really is ... attempted murder," Krista added. "Maybe Beth knows something."

"There *is* a copy machine in the back of Miscellaneous Goods. I saw it when I checked the back door," Pearla said. Max thought about the possibility for a moment before speaking.

"How would Walt have known about the article before it came out? If that was the motive, he would have taken the papers before they were distributed. The kid at the coffee shop said he got his at six this morning. I think we're being paranoid and grasping at straws." She desperately wanted an answer. She needed to know if Walt was involved and why in this sleepy little town were there two strange and possibly criminal occurrences in as many days?

Max's phone buzzed in her pocket. She checked it.

"It's the hospital," she said looking at the screen, then answered. "This is Maxine Egan, may I help you?" Max listened to the voice of the nurse on the other end as he explained, "We wanted to let you know ... Mrs. McMartin is not doing well. We're trying to reach her husband, but he's not answering his cell phone. Is he still staying at your inn? It's crucial we get in touch with him."

"I can try to locate him. I'll let him know to call the hospital right away. Thank you for the update." Max hung up and looked at her friends; she quickly relayed what the call was about. Before she could answer questions, her phone buzzed again. This time a text. It was Tyne.

Can you talk for a minute? Privately?

I'll call back, she typed.

"I need to take this call," she said to her friends and stepped outside to return his call.

"Tyne, it's Max. What's up?"

"Well, this may be a little awkward, but I thought I should tell you about last night," Tyne said. Max walked away from her cottage toward the utility shed.

"Go on."

"Colby Trawl was in here till closing. He was pretty wasted. I figured he'd walk it off, so I wasn't too concerned. It's not the first time."

"Oh," Max said. She wasn't sure what her reaction should be or why he was telling her this.

"I'm telling you because he drove home in the golf cart from your inn. I tried to persuade him to leave it in the parking lot and pick it up in the morning, but he insisted he was fine. He said he had a lot of tools and stuff and he didn't want them to get stolen. I saw a bunch of crap piled up in the back."

"But he thought it was fine to take the cart and leave it in the lot while he drank for hours," Max said sarcastically. "I actually needed the golf cart last night. I was wondering where it was." She could feel her anger rising up. How dare he take it loaded with property from her inn, and without permission. And to go get drunk, no less. Char had missed out going down to the beach last night because of him. *I should fire him. I don't owe him anything.*

Max thanked Tyne for thinking to call her. She assured him she appreciated it and that he was not overstepping. Before hanging up she had one more question.

"Tyne, do you know Beth who works at Miscellaneous Goods?"

"Yeah, everyone knows Beth. She's a character. And you don't want to get on her bad side," he said.

"Really, why?" Max asked, now quite curious about the

mysterious Beth and her disappearance.

"She's a big gossip. Loves to 'spill the tea' as they say."

Max decided not to elaborate further on why she was asking about Beth, and thankfully, Tyne didn't ask for details. She thanked him for the heads-up about Colby and ended the call, then walked over to the utility shed. The door was hanging open on the hinges. She tried to push it shut, but it was jammed. She looked inside. *What a mess.* Tools were strewn over the floor and a muddy shovel was balanced in the door jamb, preventing the door from closing. Last time she'd been in here to leave the Trawls a note, the shed was orderly. She took out the shovel and gave it a rinse with the hose, spraying her sandals in the process. She hung the shovel back on its proper hook, then closed and latched the door.

Next, Max went around to the back of the shed to check out the golf cart. It was dirty, and Tyne's description was accurate. There was a bunch of junk piled onto the backseat area. The cart had three rows. Two seats up front for a driver and passenger and two additional rows that could seat four adults comfortably, or six uncomfortably. Behind the last bench seat, there was a small space for extra items. The cart was meant to take guests to and from the shore or to give them a ride to the village or back if needed. It was really not meant as a maintenance vehicle, although Max admitted to herself, she hadn't been clear about that to the Trawls.

Max texted Pearla to join her. She wanted her advice. A minute later, Pearla was by her side.

"What should we do about this?" Max pointed at the cart. "The reason we didn't have the cart last night was Colby used it to get drunk in the village. Tyne told me.

That's what he called about." Pearla let out a disgusted sigh.

"You know my feelings. You are perfectly within your rights to let him go."

"I feel a sort of obligation towards Mr. Trawl, but not to Colby. And he's the problem," Max said.

"I agree." Pearla started removing trash from the cart: a smashed soda can, two large and empty IPA beer bottles, wadded up napkins, and a paper bag.

"Hey, that's from Miscellaneous Goods," Max said. She uncrumpled it and pulled out a receipt. "Look at this. He must have been there yesterday."

"Is there a time stamp?" Pearla asked.

"Let's see," Max said as she looked closely, before handing the slip to Pearla. "I can't see squat without my glasses."

Pearla squinted at the paper and said, "It's 6:15 p.m. Last night." Then she pulled out a blue tarp and a length of rope from the back storage box.

Chapter 22

Pearla

Was Colby Trawl smart enough to pull off a murder, yet dumb enough to leave evidence in the golf cart? Pearla turned this thought over in her mind. The answers were "no" and "yes." However, the question of *Why?* remained, and to that there wasn't an answer that was clear ... yet. Pearla sat at her small dining table. She had sheets of paper spread out and was adding notes and studying each one, determined to figure out what was happening in her new hometown. So far, she had a page for facts and pages for possible suspects, but none of it was clear and it was possible that there were not two crimes, but none. Rose had an accident, and as for Beth, it could very well turn out there was a reasonable explanation for why the shop was left open and in disarray, as well as her whereabouts. *Maybe the 'blood' was ketchup or cocktail sauce.*

Pearla's phone buzzed. It was Max. She spoke fast.

"Hey, so I got Beth's address from Tyne. We drove by her house and it was completely dark. Doors locked. Clearly no one was home. Also, Tyne said the shop stayed closed all day. I didn't exactly tell him what we saw, but there's already rumors going around."

"Take a breath," Pearla said. "Should I call the sheriff and ask what he found out?"

"No. It's after hours, and if he thinks we're being busy-bodies, he'll be less likely to share any information with us," Max said.

"True. I'm going outside for air. I'll think on it some more. We'll talk later. Or tomorrow morning."

Pearla hung up and immediately her phone buzzed again. Someone was calling from downstairs. *Maybe it's a walk-in, or someone lost their key.* No new guests were expected.

She quickly went out her main door to the second story landing and took the stairs passing through the living room and into reception. The front doors were unlocked as it wasn't ten yet. After ten, guests needed to use their provided key cards for the main outside doors. A young man stood at the reception desk. Once she looked closely, Pearla guessed he was in his early thirties, not much younger than her. He had long, golden-brown hair tied up in a man bun and light facial hair. *A hipster.* He wore brown corduroy pants, a bulky jean jacket and a shirt that looked like it was made from undyed hemp cloth. He carried an expensive leather duffle bag slung over his shoulder and Pearla knew much effort had gone into looking like he put zero effort into his appearance. She smirked, familiar with the type.

"Hi there," he said. "My name's Parker, Parker Graves. I'm meeting my girlfriend, Krista here." He extended a hand and Pearla shook it. *Of course.*

"I'm Pearla. Krista's been expecting you for a few days now." Pearla paused for a beat, then added, "What I meant to say is that she's in town having dinner with her cousin and a friend." Pearla thought she saw a flash of jealousy at the mention of a friend.

"Can you tell me where? I'll meet them there. I'd like to surprise her. I know she was expecting me sooner, but I've gotten hung up with work commitments. I feel awful about it. I want to make it up to her." His face softened, and so did Pearla's initial feelings toward him. *I shouldn't be so judgy.*

"Krista will be thrilled you're here. She's a great girl. I've gotten a chance to get to know her these last few days. Anyways, they're at Barnaby's. It's right in the village. You can't miss it."

"Thank you," Parker said, "I can map it on my phone. Do you have any vacant rooms, by the way? One near Krista's?"

"Sure. There are two small rooms on the same floor, they share a restroom, but neither room is booked, so you'd have your own restroom just down the hall. I can show you if you'd like."

"That sounds fine with me, no need to see the room." He pulled a credit card from his wallet and slid it across the counter. Pearla completed the transaction and printed a receipt which she handed him along with the brass key and key card for the common areas.

"If you leave your bags, I can take them up for you," she offered.

"There's just this one bag," he said pointing to the leather duffle he'd set on the floor. "I'd appreciate it, and thank you."

Pearla sent up a silent prayer that his intentions toward Krista were honorable. She'd been hurt too many times by good-looking snakes and didn't wish the same for Krista. She took her phone from her pocket and considered texting Max to say Parker was on the way, but the drive was so short there was no point.

After checking her email and deleting junk for a few minutes, she pulled the front doors shut and locked them. She picked up the duffle bag then went back through the living room where she switched off the overhead lights, but left a couple of small lamps lit. Upstairs, she opened the door to Parker's room with her master key. She set down his bag and heard a vibrating sound coming from it. Before she could think better of it, she unzipped the bag and looked inside. There was a phone. She picked it up and glanced at the message.

"Where are you?"

Must be Krista. But surely, he'd arrived at Barnaby's by now. It was a four-minute drive. *Why would he leave his phone?* Coming to her senses, Pearla was appalled that she'd opened a guest's bag. She returned the phone and zipped the bag shut, leaving it at the foot of the bed. She glanced around quickly, making sure the room was in order, then stepped out and closed the door, ashamed at her breach of privacy. She needed some air.

Outside in the patio area, the air was still and damp and she sat on a padded wooden bench to listen to the quiet and clear her mind. After a few minutes, her ears perked as she heard low voices and footsteps coming from the tower. The light in the tower room was off and she was planning to go there next. For now, she leaned into the shadows. There was a clear vantage point and she watched the bottom of the spiral stairs to see who was talking. The professor appeared followed by Ms. Singer. They were holding hands and walked right past her through the patio area. The downstairs rooms had doors that opened to the outside courtyard and Ms. Singer stopped at hers with the professor behind her, leaning in close. Pearla heard the key turn the lock and then they entered Ms. Singer's room. *Oh, wow. How long has this been going on?*

Just as she was about to get up, Walt McMartin came into the patio courtyard from the direction of the shore trail. He stomped his feet. *Probably getting sand off.* He knocked on his own door and stood waiting wringing his hands, and looking around furtively. The door swung inward and he disappeared into the room. Pearla knew that Roxanne's room and the McMartins' room could be accessed from the inside through the connected den.

Pearla had thought it odd when Roxanne had requested that room, and she'd suggested one of the queen rooms across the courtyard or upstairs. Now as she remained hidden in darkness, she asked herself why Roxanne was letting Walt into his own room, but she already knew the answer. *I hope Rose recovers and gets a good settlement in the divorce. And a new best friend.*

Chapter 23

Wednesday
Maxine

Char wasn't up yet, and Max wanted an early start. She hoped Char was feeling okay. She'd had more to drink than usual at Barnaby's and was slurry and unsteady by the time they'd gotten home. Max wondered if the effect of the alcohol was magnified by Char's medication. *I'll ask her about it later.*

Max left her cottage and walked over to the inn for breakfast. She waved hello to Krista who was snuggled up with Parker on one of the small sofas. They seemed happy. Neither she nor Char wanted to like Parker, but last night he'd been charming and cute, flirtatious and fun, and insistent he pay for their drinks and dinner, encouraging them to order another round. As well, he'd apologized profusely to Krista for being late to their vacation. *For now, I'll give him the benefit of the doubt.*

Max poured herself a coffee, and headed to the office to find Pearla. When she saw Walt, sitting a respectable distance from Roxanne, she remembered the phone call from the hospital and was struck with guilt. *How could I forget to tell him the hospital called?* She approached Walt and steadied her breathing.

"Mr. McMartin, did the hospital get a hold of you yesterday? They called the inn trying to locate you." Max held her fidgety hands behind her back and crossed her fingers. She didn't want to deliver the news of Rose taking a turn for the worse, and a day late, too.

"Yes, they did," Walt said. Max wondered if he planned to elaborate, but he had turned his attention back to his breakfast plate. Her need to know superseded her respect for his privacy.

"Is everything okay then?"

His voice was tinged with annoyance as he responded.

"Yes. Rose is recovering just fine." He took another bite, then added, "Thanks for asking."

"Of course. Enjoy your breakfast, and give her my best when you see her today."

"Hmmm," he said with his mouth full.

Maybe Rose's condition improved by the time they contacted him.

Max left through the front of the living room and found Pearla in the office. She was at the desk, typing, a coffee and half-eaten pastry next to her.

"I'm just filling out the data for our new employees. Their references all checked out and all three can start working whenever we're ready. Oh, and we've got more reservations coming in. This new website is so worth it."

Max relaxed. "It's going to be okay," she stated. It felt good to say it out loud. The last few days had been tense, certainly not what she'd expected.

"I know," Pearla said. "I have no doubt. There were bound to be a few bumps in the road. We've got this." Her optimism was one of the qualities Max loved most about her.

"Thanks for saying yes to this. I don't know if I could manage without you," Max said. Her phone buzzed and she glanced at the text.

"Char's in the living room. Come with me."

"Okay, I'll finish this later. I'm thinking this weekend would be a good time to train our new employees."

"Yes, let them know. We'll need the extra hands. As long as no one cancels, we're booked solid."

The two joined Char at one of the tables in the living room where Krista and Parker had already pulled over two extra chairs. As they began to discuss plans for the day, they were abruptly interrupted by Professor Lombard as he burst into the room from the outside patio. Disheveled and sweaty, he was doubled over, and out of breath.

"Call the sheriff," he puffed. "Someone needs to call the sheriff. I don't have my phone on me." All eyes were on him.

"Why, what's happening?" Walt asked. The professor spoke with authority and commanded everyone's attention.

"There's a couple with an off-leash dog. That's illegal! This shoreline is protected."

"But would that be an emergency call? I mean, they're just birds, right?" Most in the room would have enjoyed delivering a smack to Roxanne. She was too much.

"I'm calling the sheriff directly." Pearla had her phone

and was a step ahead as always.

"Couldn't you have just asked them to leash the dog?" Parker asked. Keith Lombard fixed him with a look of disdain.

"Obviously, I tried that. They ignored me. I didn't want to get into it. This is a matter for law enforcement. They can be subjected to a huge fine for damaging protected nesting areas." He ran his fingers through his hair. "God, I am so sick of people's ignorance."

Maxine was upset by it too. The Snowy Plovers were vulnerable. There were signs everywhere about keeping pets leashed. Just one dog could do so much damage, plus scare away the mother birds.

"Let's take the golf cart and confront them," she said. But then she thought better of it. "Actually, we can just walk over. When the sheriff arrives, he can take the cart. It's faster, and I'd rather not have the police cruiser messing up the trail."

"Mr. Trawl fixed the beach cruisers. Take those. Much faster," Pearla suggested.

"I'll go with you," Parker said as he got up from the table. "You shouldn't go alone."

"Sure. Good thinking," Walt added. "I don't think I'm up for an early morning bike ride, and she should have some men with her."

Ugh, such a sexist!

Max, Keith and Parker headed out to ride down to the shore. As they approached, they heard a woman's screams and sharp barking. Where the trail ended and the shoreline began, Max spotted a couple waving their hands. Their shepherd-type dog was running around excitedly as the man appeared to be trying to leash it. When the couple saw the three approach, the woman yelled, "It's a body! Our dog just found a body! Someone call the police, we can't get reception here."

"The police are on the way," Max shouted back as the three crossed the distance to meet up with the couple.

As they approached, the man finally managed to leash his excited dog. Max observed the dog straining on the leash and sniffing at what looked like a mass of seaweed rolling in and out in the shallow water of the shore. From the side of the giant ball of kelp, a slender arm and hand poked out. The woman was now hyperventilating. She sat down on a piece of nearby driftwood with her arms wrapped around her middle. She looked up with wild eyes and pointed at the professor.

"You. You were out here before yelling at us to control our dog. Is this why?" she asked, tossing her head in the direction of the human arm.

"You've got to be kidding me," Keith Lombard replied. "I'm the one who called the police." He paused, clearly trying not to lose his temper. "Because your dog is destroying protected nesting areas. Like I tried to explain before."

"Okay. Everybody settle down," Parker said as he stepped between the couple and the professor. "The police will be here soon and we'll get this figured out."

"Holy crap," he said as he bent down for a closer look at what the dog had uncovered. "Is that a...?"

Max stood back. She wasn't interested in seeing a possible body up close, the arm and hand were enough to turn her stomach and make her pulse race. Before anyone else spoke, they heard the siren of Sheriff Silva's patrol car approaching the inn. Minutes later, he pulled up in the golf cart and jogged over to the small group.

"What's going on?" he asked. Then he saw it.

"Don't touch anything!" he commanded. "I need to call for backup."

Chapter 24

Charlene

A body? Are we sure?" Charlene asked, careful to keep her voice low. Maxine was walking in slow circles around the inn's kitchen, pausing to straighten things that didn't need straightening, and to rearrange things that didn't need rearranging. Char knew her friend's quirks, Max needed to move to think. Nervous energy vibrated in the room.

"I'll be shocked if it's not a body." Max gripped the counter and leaned sideways closer to Char. "And further shocked if it's not Beth from Miscellaneous Goods."

Char was thinking the same, but hadn't wanted to voice it out loud. Beth's suspicious disappearance and the finding of a body couldn't be coincidence, but what did it all mean?

Silvermist Point was a sleepy little town and always had been. The biggest drama was gossip about who dyed their hair or whose potato salad was superior at the Fourth of July picnic, or some equally small matter.

"Not to be insensitive, but why here? Why on your property?" Char didn't want to distress Max further, but couldn't help herself from asking.

"Technically, it's not my property. No one owns the shoreline. Unfortunately, I don't think the townies will see it that way."

"They'll probably put it in that stupid newsletter," Char said. *Shut up. You're making it worse.*

"Oh, God. Of course they will. I hadn't thought of that," Max paused. "Char, do you think this will ruin me before I've even gotten started?"

Poor Max. I need to get her mind off this.

"Definitely not," Char said with more confidence than she felt. "There's no point in hanging around, waiting for news. If the sheriff plans to share anything he'll call. Let's go to Brookhaven and check out the antique shops. We can grab some lunch. You need a distraction."

"I can't. Too jumpy. I'm going to stick around here. Maybe I'll try to read or get that herb garden planted. I've got the seeds. Pearla and I need to straighten the rooms, too. But you go. I know you love to treasure hunt."

Char gathered her purse, a water bottle, and a light jacket. *Better throw in my cane, too. Just in case.* She wanted to stop at the antique store in the village before making her way to Brookhaven. The village had two shops with antiques. One was more of a vintage clothing and jewelry shop aptly named: Everything, Everything Emporium. The other, called Surroundings, held anything from old artwork, to furnishings to household items. She and Krista had explored them both on Monday. Krista had swooned over a vintage jewelry set in E.E. Emporium. The stud earrings, pendant necklace, and ring were made of pink tourmaline and diamonds set in white gold.

"These are gorgeous, don't you think? I love vintage jewelry, and pink is my favorite color stone," Krista had exclaimed.

When they inquired about origin and price, they were informed by the woman who worked there that the set belonged to the wife of one of the original settlers of the area and was at least a hundred years old.

"It's been in the shop quite a while." She opened the glass case and set the pieces on a velvet tray. "My customers always admire these pieces, but no buyer yet. I think it would make a lovely engagement set."

"Yes, it would," Krista said wistfully as she held up one of the earrings to examine it more closely.

"I can show you what the appraised value is. I have it right here." She handed Krista a printed page with the specifics of each piece.

"I'm willing to negotiate of course. Here, try on the pendant." Krista unfastened the clasp and held it up. She smiled as she looked in the mirror.

"Would you ever consider selling the pieces separately, or must it stay as a set?" Krista asked while slipping on the ring.

"Sure, I'd consider it," the shop owner replied.

"Well, let me think about it."

"Of course. But just so you know, this set is one of a kind. You won't find another like it."

Krista carefully returned the jewelry to the tray and thanked the woman for letting her try it before leaving the store.

"I just don't feel comfortable spending money. Especially on extravagances," Krista had said.

* * *

Char stepped into Everything, Everything Emporium and made her way to the jewelry case.

"Can I help you find something?" A man stood up from a wingback chair and set the book he'd been reading, along with his glasses, on the side table next to it.

"Yes, I'd like to buy the pink tourmaline set. There's a ring, earrings and necklace. My cousin and I looked at it earlier this week." Charlene moved toward the case where she'd seen the jewelry.

"Yes, yes. I know which set. Unfortunately, we only have the earrings and pendant now. The ring was sold."

"Oh, that's too bad. I was in earlier this week. I wonder when it was sold."

"I believe it sold on Monday afternoon."

I should have come back and bought it.

'I didn't think the set should be broken up, but the buyer insisted it was all they could afford. My sales associate caved and allowed the ring to be purchased by itself." The man looked at Char. She wanted to ask for details. Who bought it? A man or a woman? But it was none of her business and the owner was not giving specifics. *I don't want to seem pushy.*

"Are you still interested in the earrings and pendant?" he asked as he unlocked the case and slid open the glass panel. He put the remaining pieces on a velvet tray and held them out to Char. *They're so pretty.*

Char considered, but decided quickly. She was disappointed not to purchase the set, but said, "Yes. I'd like to buy the earrings and pendant." She handed over her credit card. The man boxed the earrings and necklace separately in dainty gold boxes. He slid the boxes into a velvet string-tie pouch.

"Would you like an additional bag?" he asked.

"No. This is fine," Char replied as she dropped the pouch into her purse.

"Thank you," she said as she walked out the door. This will be the perfect gift for Krista. It pleased her to spend money on her friends. She continued to Brookhaven with the plan to get surprise gifts for Max and Pearla as well. Bath salts? Scented candles? And maybe a little something for herself.

Chapter 25

Krista

"This. This is where I want to get married," Parker announced.

The top of the bluff had a panorama view of the dunes to the right and left and the ocean straight ahead. If you focused straight out, the view was all ocean with mesmerizing white caps marching up and crashing onto the shore. Immediately down the rocky cliff face was a tiny private beach. Private because of its virtual inaccessibility. A crude trail led down to the beach, but it was slippery and dangerous and not recommended for the general public. A sign at the trailhead warned of the possibility of getting stuck. During periods of high tide, the cliffs on either side blocked the shoreline, making it impossible to walk in either direction to connect to other beaches and trails. The only way back to the bluff was by the trail, which proved even more treacherous to traverse up than down. Other options were to wait for low tide, or be rescued by boat. Just last winter a couple got stuck at the bottom and had to be rescued by the Coast Guard.

"It's like we're on top of the world," Krista responded, the marriage comment taking her by pleasant surprise. *Don't act too eager.* This was a game with Parker, if she acted too eager, he would chastise her, no matter that it was he who had brought it up.

"Why don't we do it while we're here?" he said. "I'm sure we can find someone to officiate." Krista needed a minute to process, then the questions tumbled out.

"Married? Here? Like this week? Are you serious?"

"Sure, why not. It's what you want, isn't it?" She knew that he knew it was.

"But what about…?" Parker interrupted her and she could feel his annoyance bubbling.

Don't ruin the moment.

"Do you want to or not?"

She needed to be enthusiastic, but not overly so. "Um, yes. Sure. Definitely. I suppose Char could be my maid of honor." *I barely know her, but we're family, so…*

This was not at all what Krista had dreamed of. At the same time, it might be her best chance for love. *Has he said 'I love you?'* Parker was the only man who had ever shown a romantic interest in her. *What will I wear?* Krista snapped out of her private thoughts and threw her arms around Parker, pressing up against him and nuzzling her head on his chest. She caught a faint scent of patchouli.

"I just need to call Char. Maybe she can meet us here.

I'd like to have her help me plan." Krista broke the embrace and her fingers trembled as she took her phone from her purse. This was all happening so fast, but her lack of dating experience and her naivete kept her from peppering Parker with more questions. *He wouldn't ask me if he didn't love me.* Char didn't pick up, so Krista sent a quick text: I have news. Call me.

Chapter 26

Pearla

No guests showed up for the wine reception and Pearla wasn't sure if she should draw any conclusions from that. After the bustle of the morning with police from Brookhaven descending upon the inn and the coroner taking the body away, it had been quiet. Max had retreated to her cottage promising to call Pearla the minute she found out anything from the sheriff. Pearla had done the same. Sheriff Silva was all business as he interacted with the other officers and pointedly avoided talking to Max or Pearla.

"You might have a better shot at getting some answers," Max said. "I get the feeling Sheriff Silva might be interested in you. I see how his eyes linger a little longer than necessary."

Pearla laughed.

"No way. But I'm not above some light flirting if it gets us important information." She hoped Max wouldn't notice her face reddening. Rene was a good-looking man, and Pearla's type— if she had a type. *But he also might be a power-hungry jerk. And I've had enough of those.*

To distract herself from thinking about a woman's body being found on the beach, possibly Beth's, Pearla ran a hot bubble bath, poured a glass of wine, turned on some soft music, and took a well-deserved break. She kept her phone within reach in case the sheriff called, but she doubted he would. The slipper tub was deep, and she'd bought a bath pillow that suctioned to the back for total relaxation. Pearla placed her wine glass next to some bath brushes and scrubs on the teak tray stretched across the middle of the tub. She'd never had such a spa-like tub and she appreciated the luxury.

After a long and relaxing soak, she emerged and dried off with a thick white bath sheet. She wrapped up in her plush robe, planning to read until bedtime. Passing the window, she noticed car lights. *I hope Char had a nice day out.* Pearla gazed out her front window at the circular driveway, surprised to see cars parked out front and the small lot filled up with more. *Who do they belong to, and what are they doing here?* She glanced at the clock. *Almost 7:30. Ok, it's not that late, but when did they get here? Where are the people?*

She called Max on her cell and put it on speaker while quickly dressing and twisting her hair into a bun. No answer. As Pearla slipped on her shoes, her phone rang. Max.

"Sorry, I must have fallen asleep. Did Sheriff Silva call?"

"No, not yet. Max, there's a ton of cars out front. Any idea what's going on?"

"No, but I'll be right there. Meet you out front."

Pearla stepped into the hall on the second story. She ran downstairs to the reception area where she heard multiple voices coming from the living room. *What the heck is happening?*

Max entered through the front doors and met Pearla in the lobby.

"There are people in the living room." Pearla pointed to the double pocket doors that were closed, blocking their view of the living room. She'd never seen the doors shut before. They were always left open so the reception area flowed directly into the living room.

"Let's go through the kitchen. Maybe we can figure out what's going on before we just burst in."

"Good idea," Max replied. "This is so weird. There's nothing scheduled."

Pearla led the way, and Max followed closely behind. Pearla gently pushed the swinging door and peeked through the crack. She turned back to Max and reported in a low whisper.

"There's like ten people in there at least. Here, look." She moved aside so Max could peer in. Max took her turn.

"I see Tom and Andrew and the owner of Mama's Pizza, and I think, the lady from the post office. There are others I've seen at Barnaby's, but I don't know their names. Why is everyone here?" Pearla shrugged her shoulders and held up her hands, "No clue. Should we go in? I feel weird spying, and it's your property."

She felt a blast of hot, steamy breath on her neck and turned to find Colby right up in her personal space. He was carrying a pink pastry box and breathing heavily through his mouth.

"Excuse me," he said.

She instinctively moved away.

"Colby, what's going on?" Max asked.

"It's the monthly meeting," he said, as if that cleared up any confusion.

"And what does that mean, exactly?" Pearla was trying not to raise her voice in exasperation.

"Every third Wednesday of the month there's a meeting here."

This man is insufferable.

"A meeting for *what*?" Max's voice wavered. Clearly, she was struggling to keep her annoyance in check.

"Town concerns," Colby said as he sidestepped in front of them and entered the living room, letting the door swing closed behind him. The two women looked at each other in disbelief.

"Let's go in," Max said as she pushed the door.

Inside the space, Pearla counted ten people not including herself, Max, or Colby. Max cleared her throat loudly, then said, "Um, hi. I'm wondering what's going on here. I didn't know there was a meeting."

Instantly all eyes were on Max and Pearla. The stares felt mildly uncomfortable, but not hostile. A woman spoke up.

"It's the monthly town meeting. We always hold it here. Did the Evanses not tell you?"

"No, I'm afraid not," Max said. "But I'm more than happy to offer the space. I'll just need to calendar the dates." Then she added, "So I'm not surprised in the future."

"I'll get some coffee brewing," Pearla said. "And we'll

join you. I've been wanting to meet more people. I'm Pearla Beckett, the manager of Snowy Plover. And Maxine Egan is the new owner for those of you who haven't met her yet." Mumbled hellos and nods followed.

Max joined the group while Pearla slipped back into the kitchen where she filled the coffeemaker with water and ground coffee, then opened the large refrigerator to fetch the untouched cheese tray from earlier. While adding crackers to the tray, she heard the door swing and felt Colby's presence behind her back, again. She shook off an involuntary shudder.

"Need a hand?" he said gruffly.

Dude, personal space. She moved aside and forced a collegial smile.

"Sure. You can carry out the coffeemaker and get it plugged in. I'll grab some cups." Before he could exit back to the living room, Pearla added, "Colby, if you knew there was a meeting, why didn't you inform us? It really caught us off-guard." He offered a nod.

"Not my problem. Serves her right."

So it's Max he doesn't like. Pearla was irked. How dare he. After Max had let him keep his job.

"Why? What has she done to you, besides let you keep your position here?"

He didn't answer, just pushed through the door. Pearla plastered on a smile and followed. She joined the group, still smiling as she set down the tray of snacks and stack of extra coffee cups. Her plans for a quiet evening catching up on reading, dashed for now.

During the meeting, Pearla and Max learned that the issue of increasing publicity divided the townspeople of Silvermist Point. The business owners were interested in putting the little town on the map. Their ideas included festivals a few times a year, attracting new businesses to the village, and taking advantage of the new destination spa opening inland an equal distance from the village and Brookhaven.

"Let's give folks a reason to visit our village. Why give all the business to Brookhaven?"

"I'll tell you why. We like privacy and prefer to be passed by. Having extra tourists here spoils our coastline with noise and garbage." The man looked older. *Probably retired and doesn't need to work.*

"Yes, but you also enjoy the convenience of restaurants and groceries and shops right here in the village. We need a fair number of tourists and guests to sustain them." Max recognized the speaker as the lady who had served her at Mama's Pizza.

"All the shops have benefitted from our podcast listeners stopping in," Andrew said. Tom nodded in agreement and added, "It'd be great to fill those vacant storefronts in the village. They look bad. Not very welcoming."

"Well, personally I don't mind driving to Brookhaven. It's only thirty minutes. I don't want the extra traffic here. Strangers bring problems." The woman was not so subtly directing this comment at Max and Pearla.

"Crime and violence too, it seems," Colby said.

What the heck?

Max cleared her throat to divert the group's attention. "I realize I've only been here a short while, but believe me when I say, I only want the best for this town. It was a cherished part of my childhood. I believe more visitors to the village is a positive. Between the Snowy Plover, the new spa, and some vacation rentals, there's a limited capacity for overnight guests. Which means most of our visitors are just here for the day."

"I agree. Gracious Grapes needs new customers to stay open, and as we get more folks in the tasting room, that's what helps get the word out for our wines. People will purchase a subscription, then come back each month to pick it up. When they're here, they get a coffee or buy a book or enjoy a meal. Point is, everyone benefits."

Thank you, Marjory. I knew I liked you. Not just for your wines.

Talk dwindled into individual, quiet conversations as people helped themselves to coffee and snacks. Pearla swore she heard the mention of Beth's name, and hoped the missing woman would not become a topic of discussion. The pink box from Colby held delicate shortbread cookies which struck Pearla as mildly humorous. As she made her way around the room, she heard snippets of conversations and noted who appeared to be aligned with whom. So far, no mention of the body on the beach. *Either they're being polite, or miraculously, word hasn't spread.*

Andrew stood up and announced, "Well, we're out. We hope to see you all at our next book club meeting."

"Supporting your local independent bookstore," Andrew added cheekily to light chuckles and nods from the group.

"Would you mind opening those doors to the reception foyer on your way out?" Max asked.

When Andrew slid open the pocket doors, Pearla saw Walt and Roxanne entering from the front steps. They walked through to the living room and Walt declared, "So this is why the lot's so crowded. Did we miss something? An event?" Roxanne clasped her hands together, and sported a look of childish anticipation.

"No, this is just a meeting for the locals," Pearla said, and as soon as she did, she regretted it.

"Oh, are y'all discussing the body on the beach? Do we know who it is yet?"

Leave it to Roxanne. Janice, the postmaster, spoke up with authority, "The sheriff hasn't released that information yet."

"So it's true? They found a body? I figured it was just a rumor," a woman Pearla didn't recognize said. She had the attention of the room, and added, "My cousin said a couple was staying at the vacation rental next door to her and they claimed they saw a body on the beach and had to answer questions from the police. I didn't know she meant *this* beach."

Max shot a glance at Pearla, then spoke.

"Look, we don't have any details and it's not our place to speculate."

Everyone, just stay calm.

"Besides," Janice added, "Sheriff Silva needs to inform Beth's family before he releases her name." Unmistakable gasps followed.

Really Janice?

"Beth, from Miscellaneous Goods? Oh, no! She's been missing since yesterday. She's dead?" another man asked.

I need to learn everyone's names.

"I didn't say that." Janice was now trying to walk it back, but it was too late.

"You said exactly that," Walt countered.

"Well, none of you heard it from me. Just watch the local news at nine tonight, or maybe tomorrow morning. There should be an announcement then." Janice hastily grabbed her purse from the sofa and hurried out the patio door. The group watched her go.

"I really hope it's not Beth. She's such a kind woman, if you get to know her. I don't think she has family in the area. And she and Larry have been separated for a while now," Marjory said.

"Larry Trawl?" Max asked.

"Yes," Marjory said.

"He works here," Pearla said. "And so does his son." She looked around the room and noticed Colby was no longer present.

"He was just here." *When had he slipped out?*

Max addressed those still in the living room. As she spoke, she clicked off a table lamp. "You know what, let's call it a night. We won't get these questions answered tonight. I'm glad to meet you all, and we look forward to next month's gathering." Graciously, the remaining townspeople took the not-so-subtle cue to leave.

When they had the room to themselves again, Pearla asked Max if she could think of any reason why Colby would have an issue with her.

"Not that he likes me, but he seems to have a grudge against you," Pearla said. Max looked at her thoughtfully, and replied, "When Char and I were kids, he used to follow us around. We weren't exactly friendly with him. He was odd. Wherever we went, he seemed to lurk."

"He lurks," Pearla agreed.

"We called him, 'Cheese Troll.' Not to his face of course, but maybe he heard. We were always giggling."

"Ooh, that's harsh. He probably had a crush on you and couldn't take rejection. Most males can't."

"Okay, I admit. It was mean-spirited and I'm not proud

of it, but we were just being silly girls. Things changed when we caught him looking, or I should say peeping, in our window. We freaked out and told Char's parents. Her father complained to the owners. After this many years, you think he still holds it against me?"

"Looks that way," Pearla said.

"I'll deal with it," Max said. "And if he can't move on and treat me with respect, he'll need to find another job." *We'd probably be doing his dad a favor.*

"So, what do we think about the fact that Beth is Larry's wife?" Pearla asked.

"Estranged wife."

"That was a shock. You think he killed her?" Max's eyes popped.

"No. Do you?"

"No. I can't see it. But maybe Colby."

After tidying the kitchen, the women parted ways. Pearla was eager to get back to her book and immerse herself in fiction. *I've had enough reality today.* She stepped outside and took a deep, cleansing breath of the salty air. After tossing the trash into the bin, she moved to the stairs of the tower intending to enter her apartment by the outside door. She heard footsteps from behind and turned to see Professor Keith Lombard who was walking swiftly towards her.

"Ms. Beckett, Pearla, can I speak with you for a moment?" Pearla nodded.

"Of course. How can I help you?"

"I'd like to share some information, but I need to be assured of your discretion." He glanced around furtively. "Can we step inside the pavilion?"

"Let's go up to the tower, I was just on my way back to my apartment." After she said it, Pearla second guessed herself remembering she didn't know this man, and according to her notes, anyone and everyone was a suspect. She hesitated at the stairs, then said, "Actually, I'd feel more comfortable in the office. And let me call Max to meet us there as well." She tried to read his expression in the dark. He took a step back, increasing the distance between them.

"Okay, I understand. I'm sorry if I made you uncomfortable."

"No, not at all." *Was I that obvious?* "It's just that she's my boss, and if it concerns the inn or a guest, Max is the one to speak with. I'll just give her a quick call." Pearla dialed and got Max's voicemail. She pretended she'd reached her, and spoke into the phone, "Hey Max, do you have a couple minutes? Yes, just meet me and Professor Lombard in the office. See you in a few." She hoped Max would listen to the message and come over, but either way Keith Lombard would believe she was on her way. *Smart to be cautious.*

They entered the patio doors and went through the living room and reception where Pearla took out her key and unlocked the office. She gestured toward a seat at the table and took a seat in her office chair which was closer to the door.

"Should I wait for Max?"

"No, go ahead. How can I assist you?" Pearla grabbed a pen and notepad and looked at her phone. No message from Max.

"I trust you'll handle the information I'm about to tell you with the utmost discretion," he said.

"Absolutely," Pearla responded. He fidgeted with his sleeves, looking down. Pearla waited silently for him to spill whatever it was.

"I met Ms. Singer, and we hit it off pretty well." *I know*

where this is going. The next information came out in a rush as if he wanted nothing more than to get it off his chest.

"I spent the night with her, and when she was showering, I looked at her notes and computer. I'm so embarrassed to admit it, but curiosity got the best of me, and she'd been talking all about her process. She calls herself a method writer."

"Yes, I've wondered how that works. I know she writes romance and some erotic fiction. I must admit, I don't care for that genre." *Is he blushing?*

"But she's branching out into crime fiction and mystery. She had some notes scattered on the desk, notes about bludgeoning with various objects like bats, a rock, a block of ice. I figured maybe she got the idea from the mishap with Mrs. McMartin. Then I opened her laptop, which wasn't locked. That's when I saw notes on burying a body in beach sand."

"Oh, I see why you're telling me this," Pearla said.

"This was on Monday night and I wasn't concerned. As I said, I figured she was using the incident with Rose McMartin as *inspiration*, and the body stuff, well, that type of research makes perfect sense. I mean I can only imagine the type of twisted searches there must be in any good crime writer's search history." He looked at Pearla. *He wants to see my reaction.* She kept her expression neutral.

"Was Monday the only night you spent with her?"

"Yes, only Monday. But I didn't spend the entire night. When she got out of the shower, I made up an excuse and left. I never slept with her, if that's what you're thinking." *Why is he lying? I saw him with her last night, too.*

"So, after what happened this morning, do you think there may be a reason for concern?"

"Well, maybe. When I think of both incidents and her notes on burying a body, then a body is found…"

"Any idea of her whereabouts last night, or yesterday?"

"Not really, no. I think she was writing yesterday." Pearla said nothing, just jotted down a few notes, waiting. She picked up her phone and pretended to send a text. She was about to ask if he was certain he never saw Ms. Singer yesterday when he said, "I did see her last night, briefly. We drank some wine together in the tower room, then I followed her to her room."

"And?"

"And, nothing happened. To be honest, I was tired. I went into her room, but I left soon after. Nothing happened." Pearla speculated this could be true. She had seen them together coming from the tower. She couldn't remember seeing a bottle or wine glasses, though. *But why is he saying anything at all if he has something to hide?*

"Well thanks, Keith, for telling me. I'll be in contact with the sheriff tomorrow and I can relay this information. He's doing an investigation, so for all we know, they may already have the answer as to what happened."

"I wanted to tell someone in case it was useful. I appreciate you listening. I guess Max won't show up."

"Oh, right. She texted me and asked if we could just talk in the morning. Headache."

Chapter 27

Sheriff Silva sat in his patrol car in front of his cabin. He ran his hands through his hair and squeezed his eyes shut. *Maybe when I open them, things will be clear.* They were not. As far as he was concerned, the matter of Rose McMartin was put to rest. She'd suffered an accidental head injury. It niggled at him that he'd been so quick to judge the scene and had given Pearla the go-ahead to clean up. Pearla was an interesting woman. He wondered how old she was and if she'd ever been married or had a boyfriend. *I wonder if she finds me attractive. Never mind, I can't consider that right now. Focus.*

More pressing was the news about Beth. This would

spread. The townspeople would ask questions and look to him for answers. *I need to control the narrative.* He replayed the events of yesterday morning. Pearla had called him directly regarding a disturbance at the shoreline in front of the Snowy Plover Inn. When he saw the number with her name as contact, he'd fantasized she was looking for an excuse to get him there. The concern about a loose dog on the beach hardly seemed urgent. All the same, he'd flipped on the siren and sped over. Frankly, the body on the beach had been shocking and unexpected. Commanding authority, he'd asked everyone to step away. He'd immediately called Brookhaven, reported the emergency, and requested backup.

The image was seared in his memory. At first, only an arm and hand were visible, but judging by the bone structure and size, he knew they belonged to a woman. That it was Beth, from Miscellaneous Goods, never crossed his mind until he carefully unraveled the mass of kelp and saw her face. It shook him. Coming from the LAPD, he was no stranger to seeing deceased people, but he had never seen a person he knew, and was surprised at the rush of emotion.

Her eyes were closed; the lids were blue. He detected no visible injuries, but that would be for the coroner to decide. Following his go-to assumption that the simplest most obvious explanation was likely what happened, he conjectured this: Beth went for a walk at night on the shore and was pulled into the surf by a rogue wave. She panicked, got herself tangled in seaweed causing disorientation and was pulled under. Sadly, she drowned.

He mentally revisited the conversation from Monday evening. Beth had said someone was in the store acting strange and asking questions. He hadn't followed up the next morning as he said he would. The phone call from Pearla, summoning him to Miscellaneous Goods, had reminded him of his appointment with Beth. He'd arrived there to signs of a struggle, an unlocked store, and no Beth. But, to be fair, even if he had followed up with Beth, it would not have prevented what happened. *Or would it have?*

He thought back. How much had he revealed to Pearla and her friends? He had tried to get them out of there quickly and to exude confidence that he had the matter under control. When they left, he called the owners and asked if they'd heard from Beth. They had not. Other than that, he hadn't followed up, reasoning that an adult isn't missing until twenty-four hours have passed. Plus, no one had reported her missing. *But who would?* She just hadn't shown up for work. *I could get nailed for this.*

Beth's next-of-kin was Larry Trawl, her estranged husband. According to Janice, they were never officially divorced. Janice knew everything about the residents of Silvermist, even more than Rene let slip sometimes when he was thinking out loud. Any time he spoke with Janice about sensitive topics, he reminded her of the importance of discretion. He suspected Janice and Beth were the co-authors of *The Silvermist Point of View,* but he had never specifically asked either one. *Best I don't know—conflict of interest.*

He placed a call to Larry Trawl who did not answer. Rene put the patrol car into gear and drove to Larry's trailer on the outskirts of the Snowy Plover Inn property. He decided to approach from the back, to avoid any extra attention. Tall stands of eucalyptus trees created a nice cover. It was still early and Rene hoped Larry would be home. Showing up at the inn, again, was not ideal. They would pepper him with questions for which he had no answers.

He navigated the fire road around the back of the property and pulled up near the rickety trailer. This was the first time he'd seen it up close. The trailer was thirty feet long, rusty and dented. A set of makeshift wooden stairs led to a sliding glass door with a torn screen, while a faded fabric awning supported by spindly metal legs hung listlessly off the side of the structure. Two lawn chairs were positioned near a smoldering fire pit. Rene took this as a sign that he'd find Larry Trawl at home. He got out of his vehicle and approached the steps.

"Mr. Trawl, are you home? It's Sheriff Silva. I need to speak with you." He paused and waited, hearing noises from within and the slider opened. Larry Trawl lifted the screen out of the frame and stepped onto the small landing at the top of the wood stairs. He said nothing, but offered a scowl.

"Good morning, Mr. Trawl." He paused, waiting for a response, and when none came, he continued. "You may have heard yesterday that a body was found on the shore near this property." Larry fixed him with a stare and raised one bushy eyebrow.

"Yes, my son mentioned it."

"I'm sorry to be the one to tell you, but we believe the deceased is your wife, Beth. I need you to come to the hospital and identify the body." He gave him a minute to process the information. "I realize this is a shock, and I can drive you if you prefer."

Larry Trawl bowed his head and responded in a whisper. "Beth? She passed away?" The old man's shoulders slumped. He took in a sharp breath.

Rene could feel his grief. Noises emanated from inside the trailer and Rene watched as Colby Trawl stepped out the single door near the front. One hand was inside his shirt and he was scratching his armpit.

"What's this about? Hi, Sheriff. I haven't done anything. Been on my best behavior." His rumpled appearance and bloodshot eyes told a different story.

"Shut up, Son. This is serious. The sheriff says something happened to Beth." Larry choked on a sob. "He thinks it was her body on the shore. I'm gonna need to identify her."

Rene watched for Colby's reaction. *Was that a smirk?*

"Sorry Pop, I don't know what to say. She hated me, though." He stepped back into the trailer, then reappeared with a cigarette and lighter. He moved away from the trailer before lighting up. *Still close enough to hear us.*

"I'll go myself to identify Beth. There's no need for you to drive me."

"Sure, I understand. I have a few questions if you're up for it. It shouldn't take long." Rene flipped open his notepad and clicked his pen.

"Is this official?" Larry asked. "Because I had nothing to do with this, ya know." He wiped a stray tear with the back of his sleeve.

"I've always loved her. She was my second wife." He lowered his voice. "My first wife, the boy's mom," he jutted his chin toward Colby, "we never got along. Oil and water. She passed away 'bout ten years ago."

"I'm sorry, sir. As I said, just a few questions, if you don't mind."

"Sure, okay."

"Do you have any idea why Beth would be out walking

the shoreline at night? Specifically, Monday night?"

"No, I don't know why she would go there alone. It was our special place when we were together. We used to love to walk in the early evening. She'd come pick me up at work, and we'd walk down, sometimes have a picnic. Maybe she was thinking of me." He choked on a sob. "I never should have left her. She was alone in that house, and I'm stuck here in this broken-down trailer."

"Why'd you leave?" Rene thought he knew the answer, but wanted Larry's version.

Larry sighed. "Beth and Colby never got along. She wouldn't let him stay. So, I moved with him into the trailer."

"With all due respect, may I ask why you live here too, rather than with your wife? This can't be comfortable."

"I have to monitor him. I've failed him too many times in his life. Guilt, I suppose."

"He loves me more than he ever loved her," Colby shouted. Evidently, he'd been listening in. "That, and he doesn't trust me to make good choices for myself."

This guy is a grown man.

"How old are you, Colby?" Rene asked, since he was inserting himself into the conversation.

"I'm 53, officer!" Rene could hear the sneer in Colby's tone and struggled not to react in a juvenile way by making an "L" sign with his fingers over his forehead. Either that, or laugh at the absurdity.

"See? He never knows when to keep his trap shut. That mouth gets him in trouble. Has his whole life." He faced Colby. "You better get over to the inn and check the list, get started. I won't be over till later." Colby nodded and began walking toward the inn with the swagger of an obnoxious middle school boy.

Rene Silva had never been in a serious relationship, and at times wondered whether he was missing out on having a wife and kids, but this exchange made him feel good that he was single and unattached. He needed to steer the topic back to Beth.

"When was the last time you saw Beth, or spoke with her, Larry?"

"I saw her in town on Saturday. I came into the shop and we spoke. It was a friendly conversation. She knows I still love her, but doesn't understand the choice I made. That's the last I spoke with her. She called me Monday though, and I missed it. Odd for her, she didn't leave a message."

"What time was the call? That may be important." Larry checked his phone.

"It was 5:43."

Hmm, right before she called me.

"Did you have any other contact?"

"No. I tried to reach her yesterday. She never responded. Now I know why."

"Thanks, Larry. That's all I have for now. Again, I'm so sorry for your loss. Please call if you remember anything you think is important. It'd be useful to figure out why she was on the beach alone."

"Well, she did like to walk down there, but only in the daylight. Unless the moon was full. Or, when she had a friend with her, or me, when things were good between us. She was afraid of the tides. The moon was full Monday night, so it would have been well-lit. Maybe she missed me. That's what I think. And I wasn't there to save her." He was crying now and not trying to hide it. His shoulders heaved and he swiped his eyes with the cuff of his shirt.

"I could have saved her. Protected her."

Rene gave him a couple awkward pats on the back then turned toward his patrol car. As he maneuvered slowly back out on the dirt road, a call came through and he pulled over. He listened intently as the medical examiner reported his findings. The medical examiner had determined the official cause of death for Beth was drowning. However, there were significant bruises on her shoulders indicating she had been forcefully pushed under water. There was also a large bruise and cut on the back of her head. A broken finger nail indicated signs of her fighting back, but no DNA evidence was likely to be found given that her body was in the water for at least twenty-four hours and probably more.

"Thank you for the information," Sheriff Silva said. "And after I look at the report, I'll call if I need any additional clarification." He hung up. *Why would Beth be a target for murder?* He wished he'd not shared with Pearla and the other ladies that he had an appointment with Beth the morning she was discovered missing, an appointment he'd failed to show up for. *Would it have changed the outcome though?* If he was honest with himself, he should have gone over to speak with her when she'd called the night before. Now he wondered if he'd been negligent in his duties. He certainly did not want to think of someone ending up dead because he needed to get home to his cat, steak, and whisky, not necessarily in that order.

As he drove, an idea struck him. He pointed his car in the direction of the village. He would stop in at Miscellaneous Goods. When he arrived, he was pleased to see the store was void of customers. The young man working was on his phone behind the counter, but set it down when he noticed Rene. It was business as usual.

"Hi Sheriff, how can I help you? I heard about Beth. It's so sad."

"Well, yes. Were you the one who cleaned up on Tuesday?"

"I was."

"And your name is?"

"Stone," he said and his lip twitched. *What is with the naming of people after inanimate objects?*

"Was there anything missing? Did you notice anything out of the ordinary?" Rene avoided eye contact. These were questions that should have been covered when Beth was only missing, not dead. Now she was dead. Was it too little too late? If the worker was judging, he didn't show it.

"No, nothing was missing, not even cash. I don't think the owners filed a report or an insurance claim. There were a few broken jars and bottles of wine, but no real damage. The truth is, Beth was known to have a volatile temper. We all assumed she got angry and threw down the bottles herself then stormed out."

"So something like this has happened before?" The wheels were spinning in Rene's brain and he waited patiently to hear more. *Let him talk.*

"Once before. That son of her ex could really get her fired up. Last time she lost her cool it was because of him. She threw a jar of pickles at his head. Missed. Then he threatened to have her arrested for assault. I feel bad now, but when I saw the store and heard she was missing, I figured she just stormed off and needed to cool down. I had no idea she'd turn up dead. And I'll swear to that." *Poor kid thinks I'm here to arrest him.*

"There was no way you could have known." Then,

keeping his tone light and as casual as possible, "Say, is there a security camera?" He didn't want to sound obvious. He should have checked the camera before now. *Not my fault. Everything happened so fast, and I don't have anyone else. I can't think of everything.*

"Yes, follow me. The monitor's in the storage room." Rene followed him to the back of the store.

"Let's take a look and see who was in here on Monday," Rene said.

Stone turned on the monitor.

"Lemme see if I can remember how to use it." He fiddled around typing in commands. "All I'm getting is a black screen. Hmm, it might be broken. I haven't looked at this in ages. It might not even work. The owners have the 'Smile, You're On Camera' sign posted as a deterrent for shoplifters, but that's never been an issue."

"Where are the cameras positioned?" Rene asked. "Let me have a look at them." Stone showed him the camera above the register and explained, "There's only this one, it's a wide angle, with a view of most of the store." He dragged a tall stool over and climbed up, then stood on the counter. He looked down at the sheriff.

"The lens has been spray painted," Stone reported.

Great. Wonder when that happened.

Stone jumped down from the counter top. A couple of older ladies came in and he asked if they needed help finding anything. They declined, going straight to the wine selection, each grabbing a bottle. Stone rang them up and they left.

"I'll take another look at the camera program; I can probably figure out how long it hasn't been recording."

"I'll wait here," Rene said and began to wander around

the store, hoping to find some clue though he didn't know what he was looking for. He filled a basket with artisan pasta and spicy sauce. He also found some garlic croutons that looked good, as well as a bottle of red blend wine, nothing that could spoil in the trunk as it would be hours till he could kick back and relax at home. Doom settled like a heavy cloud when Stone informed him that all the footage from Sunday forward was black screen.

"What about before that?" he asked, doubting it would be of any use.

"Deleted," Stone said. "All of it, deleted."

Rene wanted to shout the F-word at the top of his lungs, but he was a gentleman, and a professional. He calmly paid for his merchandise and took his receipt. On his way out, he called, "Thanks for your help, Stone. I'll be in touch."

Chapter 28

Larry Trawl

L arry Trawl had never seen a deceased person before. The few funerals he had attended featured closed caskets. Not that it would have made a difference. Nothing could have prepared him to see Beth, the woman he still loved intensely, lying on a metal gurney and covered in a thin sheet. He was still processing the shock of finding Rose McMartin in the cellar, whom at first, he believed was dead.

When the attendant grasped the sheet and slowly pulled it back, Larry sucked in a breath and nodded to the man indicating that, yes, it was Beth. He signed some papers and was then asked by a friendly receptionist if he needed a minute. She handed him a Styrofoam cup of black coffee and he sat in a plastic chair trying to gather himself before leaving. Thoughts of regret were like an unpleasant weighted blanket. *Was this my fault?*

He felt deep in his gut that Colby wasn't capable of such a horrific act, but a sliver of doubt plagued him. Who else knew that Beth liked to walk the shore at the full moon besides him and his son? And Colby had always disliked Beth. He resented her for kicking him out, even though she had tried to tolerate him and had given him multiple chances to follow the few rules she insisted upon.

Beth didn't drink alcohol, having grown up with a raging alcoholic, and insisted that no alcohol ever be in her house. That was fair. But Colby had bent the rules by drinking elsewhere and arriving home stinking drunk and belligerent. It was her house, hers and Larry's, that Larry had worked years to be able to afford. He recalled the day Beth had snapped, saying she couldn't live like this anymore, wouldn't live like this anymore. So Larry left with his son rather than stay with his wife and was never able to explain to Beth, or even to himself, why he felt it was his duty as a father.

Larry sent Colby a text to call immediately. He wanted answers. Colby called back. Larry struggled to keep his voice level and calm.

"Where were you Monday night?"

"Oh, hi, Dad," Colby deadpanned. "Why?"

"Colby, Beth is dead and I need to know what happened to her."

"So, you think I had something to do with it? Are you kidding me?"

"I assure you, Son, this is no joke. Where are you? You need to go somewhere you can speak privately and not be overheard." Larry could hear some shuffling and clanging.

"I'm in the shed. No one's around."

"Okay, just check outside. I don't need anyone overhearing your side of this conversation."

"Coast is clear, Dad. Monday I was at Barnaby's. And before you ask, yes, I was drinking, but not too much, just stopped in for a beer or two and a shot. That place was hoppin' Monday night."

"When, and how, did you get home?"

"I don't remember the exact time. Whenever Barnaby's closed. I stayed till last call, then drove the golf cart back."

Larry sighed before responding, "Yes, I know. Max complained about that. She needed the cart Monday night and it wasn't there. You didn't have permission to take it off the grounds. It's for work purposes only, not for you to go out partying."

"Those ladies are so uptight. What is it with middle-aged women? I think they're obsessed with me."

Larry chose to hold his tongue about this ridiculous comment and stick to the topic.

"Focus, Colby. So are you saying Barnaby's is the only place you went on Monday, other than the inn and our trailer?" The kid needed things spelled out explicitly. He was never the sharpest tool.

"Look Dad, I know what happened to Beth. And it wasn't me."

Larry waited a few seconds for him to elaborate, then shouted, "Talk!"

"Before I went to Barnaby's, I was at Miscellaneous Goods where Beth works, well, worked. You know the woman who got clocked on the head? Her husband was there too. Same time as me. He heard me telling Beth that the accident at the inn was no accident."

"But why would you say that to her?" Larry asked, confused.

"I was trying to get back in her good graces. I figured she might look kindly on me if I gave her some juicy news for the Silvermist Point of View."

"How did you figure out she was one of the writers? It's supposed to be anonymous."

"I have my ways. I'm not as stupid as you think. Plus, I learned a few things when I was locked up, and I can read people pretty well. It's one of my many talents."

"I don't understand, Colby. If you've known all along it was the woman's husband who tried to kill her, why in the world would you keep it quiet?"

Colby's explanation came out in a rush as if the whole conversation was nothing but a bother and an interruption to his day.

"I didn't know. I was bluffing! Just trying to give 'ole Beth a tidbit for her newspaper. Then I saw Walt's reaction. He went white as a sheet; the man had guilt written all over him. I followed him out and the other woman, the couple's so-called friend, was in his car. Then I knew for sure; couldn't make out the words, but it was a dog fight in there. He must've come back later and, I don't know, kidnapped Beth, taken her to the beach and drowned her? I can't figure out everything. Beth had already written the article though, so he killed her for nothing. Now can I get off the phone before those ladies accuse me of wasting time? They left a list of stuff for me to do, and you're taking the day off, so…"

What was wrong with this kid?

"Colby, you're going to need to speak with the sheriff."

"No. I won't. Let him figure it out on his own. As for

me, I'm carrying a knife and staying away from that man, just to make sure I'm not next on his hit list."

Larry was too exhausted to argue. He needed to mourn Beth and the life they could have had were it not for Colby. He found himself in the driveway of his and Beth's house, having no memory of how he'd arrived there. He'd not been inside since the day he and Colby moved out. He'd wanted to respect Beth. As she saw it, he'd chosen a derelict son and broken-down trailer over her. He was shocked his old key still worked, certain she'd have changed the locks. The house smelled of her perfume. He checked the closet and saw his clothes were still there, untouched. Beth had threatened to donate them if he didn't come get them.

"Go ahead," he'd said. "There's no room in the trailer, and I don't need nice things anymore."

"You know you don't have to do this," she pleaded.

"There's no other way, Beth. I'm sorry. I wish you'd understand, but I don't blame you if you don't." Eventually Beth's sadness shifted into contempt and the silent treatment. After six months they would nod or exchange simple pleasantries if they encountered each other, but nothing more. It was a stalemate. Neither willing to budge, though both were unhappy with the situation.

Larry dared not return to the trailer. *No reason I can't sleep here.* He feared his anger would get the best of him. He couldn't deal with Colby's cavalier attitude when the love of his life was gone. Not today. Neither would he call the sheriff. He wanted some time to clear his head. And a good, stiff drink.

In the back of his closet, he slid the hidden panel to reveal his secret stash of alcohol. He grabbed the bourbon, took it to the kitchen where he stood for a moment. Beth had chosen this kitchen, replacing the pea green appliances and gold Formica with maple cabinets and stainless-steel appliances. Larry was pleased to make it just as she requested. It was a peaceful life, before the disruption of Colby moving in. Larry poured a large glass, all the while hoping for a miracle that Beth would walk through the door.

Chapter 29

Pearla

Pearla received an alert on her cellphone that a reservation request was made on the website. She logged in on her way to the office. The name was Bella McMartin, and she'd left a contact number. Pearla called immediately.

"I'm calling back from Snowy Plover Inn regarding a reservation request."

"Yes. My name is Bella. My parents are staying at your inn and my mom had an accident. I'm on my way to the hospital to check if they'll discharge her. We'll stay in Brookhaven tonight then come to your inn on Friday and we'll plan to check out Saturday, as long as Mom's up for it. Anyway, I tried to reserve the room adjoining my parents, but it's marked unavailable. Can I get that room?"

Pearla thought quickly. "Must be a glitch in the system. I'll figure it out, but yes, it's available. I'll reserve that room for you for tomorrow." Pearla wanted to keep her on the line. *Did this daughter have any idea what was going on with her parents who seemed headed for certain divorce?*

"Oh, thank you," Bella said. "I'm anxious to see my mom. Dad insists she's fine, says there's no reason for me to come, but I haven't spoken to her directly and I'm concerned the hospital is holding her for so long. I think he's downplaying her injuries so as not to worry me. He tends to make light of things. Sorry, I'm rambling." She paused. "But, before I hang up, can you give me any more insight about what happened? Are you familiar with my parents? I understand the accident happened at the inn. Dad says it was just a mild concussion."

Pearla chose her words strategically. She did not want to lie.

"It's my understanding that she suffered a concussion. A heavy oil can fell from a shelf, and unfortunately, she was in the wrong place at the wrong time."

"Exactly where was she that a heavy can could fall on her?" This was what Pearla was afraid of. *Have I said too much?*

"We think she must have taken a wrong turn. She ended up in the basement we use for storage. It's off-limits to guests. The stairs are quite narrow. She grabbed a shelf and…"

"That's awful," Bella said. "I've noticed her memory has been slipping. Poor Mom." Pearla quietly let out a breath. Bella was not placing blame. This was good. She had not had to lie.

"Well, if there's nothing else I can help you with, we look forward to seeing you Friday. You can check in at any time. I'll have the room all ready for you." Bella thanked her and hung up.

Now I need to get Roxanne out of that room.

Pearla tapped lightly on the door of Roxanne's room. She strained to listen for footsteps.

"Roxanne? Are you there?" she called. A look down at the parking lot from her upstairs window had confirmed that Walt had left. His car was gone. The question remained whether Roxanne was with him, or here on the grounds. Her car was in the lot. If Pearla could get her to move to a different room, she could prepare the room for the McMartins' daughter and avoid a potentially awkward situation. She knocked once more and a bit louder.

"I'm coming, I'm coming. Hold your horses!" Roxanne's shrill tone emanated from within. She opened the door forcefully and said, "What? What is it?"

"Sorry to bother you. I hate to inconvenience you, but the McMartins' daughter, Bella, is checking in tomorrow and she has requested this room to be close to her parents." Pearla kept her voice level and her expression neutral. She never knew what to expect with Roxanne.

"And you want me to move?" Roxanne raised an eyebrow.

"Yes, please. You can choose any of the other available rooms. None are booked until Sunday."

"Sure. Okay. I'll move." Roxanne's face was difficult to read.

"We'll comp the last night for you, as a thank you for your flexibility," Pearla added. "If you gather your belongings, I'll relocate them for you. I'll bring over a cart. Would an upstairs room be okay?" Pearla spoke quickly, realizing she didn't want Roxanne to reconsider.

"Sure. Just give me the nicest room you have. And throw in a bottle of wine from your cellar as well, for my trouble. I'd like the Gracious Grapes label, the Chardonnay."

How does she know I have that wine? I've never served it.

"You can get my things in fifteen minutes. I'll stop by the reception desk for my new key on my way out."

"Thank you for being so accommodating. I'll have it all ready for you when you return." *That went as smoothly as could be expected.*

After Roxanne collected her new key and drove off, Pearla rolled the luggage cart to the room. She hadn't been in either room since before the McMartins and Roxanne checked in last Saturday. Twice they'd asked for fresh towels, which Pearla had brought straightaway and exchanged the fresh towels for the used ones, never entering either room. Neither Walt nor Roxanne had made the request to have their room cleaned. Just as well because she'd been plenty busy with other matters. The new staff members would help her prep the rooms for the next round of occupants on Saturday morning. *Once this group leaves, I can stop worrying about Rose's close call and Beth's death. I'll leave that to the sheriff. After I share what information I've gathered.*

Pearla loaded Roxanne's three suitcases onto the cart. They were heavy and she didn't want to lug them upstairs, but the inn was not equipped with an elevator and she'd already promised her the upstairs room. It wasn't the nicest room, but Roxanne did not deserve the nicest room, and Pearla was okay with being petty about it. She could ask one of the Trawls to move the luggage, but the less interaction with them the better as far as she was concerned, especially Colby. His presence set off alarm bells in her nervous system.

Chapter 30

Maxine

Pearla reminded Max they planned to host a gathering around the fire pit where guests could sip wine or hot chocolate and roast marshmallows, if they wished. It was to be a regular Thursday night event. Max was hardly in a head space to host anyone other than close friends, but when darkness fell, she and Pearla lit the fire and were soon joined by Krista, Parker, Char, Keith and Ms. Singer. Max appreciated Walt and Roxanne were not in attendance, bringing their gift of awkward interactions.

Keith, Char, and Parker were comparing notes on the various countries they'd visited. Parker was almost as well traveled as Char, having visited an impressive number of cities, while Keith's adventures were focused on bird habitats in more out-of-the-way rural locations all around the globe. After the three had dominated the conversation for an hour, while everyone listened attentively in quiet fascination, Ms. Singer, sitting on the opposite side of the fire pit from Keith, interjected, "Maxine, can you tell us what you know about the resident ghost?"

Way to change the subject.

"Not too much. It's just a local legend Char and I were fond of as girls. I doubt there's any truth to it." Maxine was not sure if she believed in ghosts. The church did not take a definite stance on the matter, though ghosts were generally believed to be the spirits of those who had died but might be stuck in a state of purgatory. This didn't make sense to Max if Amelia, resident ghost, was a child. Perhaps the spirit was of someone else, if there was a spirit at all. Max recalled the cold feeling from Monday morning. All the ladies had felt it. It was not a natural breeze.

"Well, what do you know about it?" Ms. Singer asked again. "I'm always interested in new material for my stories." Pearla, who was sitting next to her, gave Max a double nudge. Max took a deep breath, but Char spoke first.

"So, the belief is that Amelia lived here with her parents. She drowned in the ocean one night while out exploring the shoreline admiring the full moon. It was a tragedy," Charlene explained.

"Interesting," Ms. Singer said. "I've always heard it said that ghosts stay near the place of their death if there's unfinished business, especially if their death was no accident. Maybe she was murdered." She sat back in her Adirondack chair. Everyone stared at the dying embers of the fire until Parker spoke up.

"Now there's a second death on the very same shoreline.

Clearly, the only explanation is that the woman was lured into the ocean by the ghost of the girl."

"Exactly what I was thinking," Ms. Singer said excitedly. "You'll probably have two resident ghosts now. Makes for an intriguing tale, I'd say."

"Is it just me, or does this conversation seem disrespectful? I mean, a woman just died. I'm sure she has friends and family who are devastated. They wouldn't want strangers making jokes," Krista said.

"It wasn't meant to be a joke, but okay." Ms. Singer unceremoniously stood gathering her cloak around her. "I'm going to bed. Even with the fire, it's too cold out here. I should have worn a beanie." The others mumbled their good nights as she left.

"I think I'll take a swim and soak in the hot tub, if anyone cares to join me," Char said.

"We will," Krista volunteered herself and Parker. "Meet you there." They left. Pearla, Keith and Max remained.

"See, I told you she was suspicious," Keith said.

"Who? Ms. Singer?" Max asked.

"Yes." Keith turned to Pearla. "Did you tell Max what I found on her computer? I wouldn't be surprised if she's the one who killed Beth." Keith was flustered, but then his tone switched to anger and he took a step towards Pearla. "You never called the sheriff, did you? Why not?"

"I wasn't able to get a hold of him. He hasn't gotten back to me."

Max picked up on Pearla's unease and stepped between them asking, "Why didn't you call him yourself if you had concerns or something to report?"

He shook his head as if to clear his thoughts, then ran his fingers through his hair. When he spoke this time, his tone was softer, "Sorry, ladies. That was unfair. I'm not used to this kind of drama. I think I'll pack my bags and head out, first thing."

"Oh, you don't need to leave. Don't let it spoil your trip. You're booked till Saturday," Max encouraged.

"Thanks. I'll see how I feel in the morning." And with that he started walking away, but turned back calling out, "Do you need a hand putting out the fire? You shouldn't leave it hot."

"No, we've got it. Thank you though," Pearla said, waving him off. When he was out of earshot she said, "Good thinking keeping him here. He was acting suspicious."

"So was the author," Max mused.

"I don't know what to believe at this point. And I never put a call in to Sheriff Rene. I feel like we should let him do his job, but is he? Don't we have a right to know what's happening with the investigation? We should be given that courtesy, since both of the incidents occurred here."

"Oh, so it's 'Sheriff Rene' now?"

"Shut up Max. This is serious."

"Ugh, don't remind me." Max dumped sand on the fit pit. After extinguishing the embers completely, the two women hefted the heavy lid and set it on the sunken pit. Then they walked to Max's cottage. Max boiled water for some herbal tea and they discussed whether to call Sheriff Silva to relay their concerns. Both agreed it was time to check in.

"I'll put it on speaker, but you talk," Max directed. She dialed Rene Silva's cell number. She didn't know if it was a personal number or if it was an official one. He picked up on the third ring.

"Sheriff Silva here."

"Yes, Sheriff, this is Pearla Beckett and Max Egan from Snowy Plover Inn."

"Of course. What can I do for you so late at night?" Max nudged her and raised her eyebrows. Pearla silently mouthed, "Stop" and suppressed a nervous giggle.

"Would you mind stopping by the inn tomorrow morning? Maxine and I would like to share some information we've been gathering. Honestly, it might prove to be nothing, but I think we should talk. In person." She paused to let him respond.

"I was thinking the same. I have some questions I'd like to ask you. I was out this morning at your caretaker's trailer. I needed to inform him about Beth's death. She was his estranged wife. Not sure if you ladies knew that."

"Yes, we did hear that. It's terribly sad. How do you think it happened?"

Max gasped. "Pearla, you can't ask that!" she whispered.

Pearla shrugged and mouthed, "Why not?" Rene cleared his throat.

"Well, that's proprietary information. I'm not at liberty to say. But you can rest assured. I've got everything under control. I can probably tell you more tomorrow. You understand." This was a statement rather than a question, but he didn't sound angry, more like frustrated.

"Right. I get it. So, what time can we expect you tomorrow?"

"Around eleven. I have business with the Brookhaven Police Department."

"Okay, we'll see you then."

Pearla left shortly after and Max got into her pajamas. She was headed to bed, when she heard her phone vibrate from the bedside table. The message was from Krista.

can u check on C?

she is still in the hot tub

Max wondered why Krista would send such a message, but she immediately responded with a thumbs up, tugged on her boots, and headed to the hot tub, unconcerned to be seen in her pajamas. Passing the pool, she called out to Charlene. The bubbles were off and steam rose in a plume from the hot tub. Char's head was lolling and her neck was bent at an awkward angle. Max ran the last distance, calling Char's name. She grabbed her shoulders and shook her. Char's body was limp.

"Char. Char. Oh my God. Are you okay?"

"Hmm," Char mumbled. "I must've passed out."

Max picked up the empty stemless plastic wine glass. *It's not like her to over indulge.* "Can you stand?" she asked her friend. "Here, let me help you." She hooked her elbows under Char's armpits and straightened her to a more upright position. "Push up with your legs."

Char half stood then sat on the edge of the hot tub. After getting her bearings, she swung her legs out of the tub then fully stood as Max supported her. Max guided her to a nearby lounger and helped her into her robe. Then she sat next to her gently rubbing her back.

"Let's get these flip flops on you. Girl, how much did you drink?"

"I didn't. Well not much." Charlene groaned and bent over at the waist. "I'm gonna be sick." She stood and took a few unsteady steps toward the surrounding bushes. Max followed.

"I'll hold your hair."

"Like the good old days," Char laughed weakly, then vomited into the bushes.

Max walked her back to the cottage and to her room. She left a pitcher of water on the nightstand with a glass and asked if she'd be okay, to which Char muttered a barely coherent, "Yes." Then Max shut the door, but not all the way.

Chapter 31

Friday
Maxine

How's Char? Is she up yet?" Max read Krista's text and responded, "Not yet, I was just going to check on her." Maxine crept stealthily down the hall to look in on her friend. She eased open the door to Charlene's room. Butters rushed past and jumped onto the bed. All Max could see was a rumpled swimsuit on the floor and a lump of twisted blankets and sheets on the bed. Soft snoring emanated from under the pile. *Okay, she just needs to sleep it off.* Butters began kneading the lump and purring.

Seeing her friend like this was a bold reminder of their shared past. There were so many times in their youth that the two of them drank too much, acted regrettably, and had needed to sleep it off, but once Maxine had a husband and a child to consider, opportunities to let loose as she had as a young adult were few and far between. When Sawyer grew old enough where Max felt comfortable leaving him with Adam for a night or two, the friends made a point of having a girls-only weekend once a year. Sometimes Pearla or other friends would join them and they'd reminisce. Those who were married with young kids could temporarily unlock and step away from the shackles of their day-to-day responsibilities.

Charlene had never had to be responsible for anyone but herself. Even when her parents were aging and needed assistance, she could hire top round-the-clock care which hardly affected her own social life. Not that she wasn't a devoted daughter, she was. Max and Char's friendship was a paradox, two very different personalities and life paths, but both women loved and respected each other. Maxine, craving stability, needed to be anchored. She sought ways to be responsible and grounded. She enjoyed being a caregiver to her son and her husband. Char enjoyed freedom and balked at the notion of being tied down to any person or location. But the second either of the women needed the other, they were there for each other without hesitation. When Adam passed away, Char had quietly moved in with Max and stayed for weeks.

Max leaned on the door frame and watched her sleeping friend. *What if Krista hadn't texted last night?* But she had, and now Char was safe and sleeping off what Max supposed would be a brutal hangover.

As Max stood peeking in, she wondered why Char had gotten so sick the previous night. It was very out of character. With all the medications she was on, Char never had more than one or two drinks. Max couldn't recall seeing her drunk in the last fifteen years. Tipsy, maybe, but not drunk. *Except for Tuesday*. It must have been a reaction, or maybe she was ill with the flu.

"Char. Are you feeling better?" Max waited for a response. "Can I make you breakfast?"

A rustling from the bed, and then, "Ugh. I feel terrible. I'm not sure I can stand up. I'm so dizzy." She reached out a hand to pet Butters.

"Char, you scared me. You were so out of it when I found you, I thought maybe you drowned."

"I only had two glasses of wine at the fire pit, and I drank iced tea at dinner before that. Then when we were in the hot tub, I had champagne." Char had still not fully emerged from under the tangled bed covers.

"That doesn't sound like too much. Do you remember when I pulled you from the hot tub?" Max asked.

Char sat up and placed her hands on either side of her head as if to steady it. She blinked a few times. Her auburn hair was a matted mess and her eyes were smudged with mascara. She reached for the water carafe on the side table and poured a glass, then gingerly took a sip.

"Why champagne? You've never liked it," Max said as she sat down on the bed. Char sat fully up and turned to her, eyes wide.

"Max. Krista and Parker are getting married! He proposed yesterday. They told me in the hot tub. We were toasting with champagne he'd brought. I don't know how I feel about it. Do you think it's too soon?" Max thought for a minute. "If I remember correctly, they haven't been together very long. Seems soon, but you shouldn't say anything unless she asks. He's a nice guy from what I can tell. And she's wild about him."

"That's true. But Krista doesn't have any real relationship experience. He's her first serious boyfriend. She confided to me that he hasn't said, 'I love you' yet, and now a proposal? It just feels … too fast." Char laid back down. "I feel awful. The room is spinning. I think I might be sick again." Max grabbed the plastic trash can she'd left by the bedside and handed it to Char. "You don't look well. Maybe it's a virus. I think you should take it easy today."

"I don't think I have a choice. I'll rest a little more, then get some coffee and toast. If I skip my coffee, I'll get a brutal headache."

"Okay. If I see Krista, I'll let her know you're under the weather and taking it easy today. Should I say congratulations? Or is the engagement a secret?"

Char looked thoughtful. "You know, I don't know. Best not to mention it until they do. He didn't give her a ring yet. I sense it was spur of the moment."

"Got it." Max's phone buzzed, and she glanced at the screen.

"It's Pearla," she said as she was walking out. "I'll check on you a bit later. Call if you need anything." Max closed the door, then slid her finger across the screen to answer.

"Hey, what's up? Is the sheriff early?" she asked Pearla.

"No, but the IT guy is here. I completely forgot we booked an appointment."

"Shoot. Me too. I was supposed to be practicing how to access the cameras and use the remote functions for the lights and pool filters. He's gonna need to give me another lesson. I don't suppose you've tried it out either?"

"Nope. I think we've both been distracted by more pressing matters," Pearla said, and was quickly interrupted by Max, as realization dawned.

"Oh my gosh, Pearla!"

"We have video cameras!" the two women shouted in unison.

"Do you know what this means?" Max asked excitedly.

"That we might have footage we can use from Sunday night," Pearla said. "Come to the office."

"I'm on the way."

Minutes later the two women were sitting with Eric in the office, crowded around the computer monitor. The last time he'd been here, Max had felt as if her brain would explode. She was never good with electronics of any kind. It had taken forever to learn the various platforms needed for teaching and she had often reverted to using the actual textbook rather than the online version and having her students submit handwritten assignments. *At least they couldn't cheat as easily.*

"We'd like to review how to see the security camera footage, please," Pearla requested. Max grabbed a notepad. She was determined to learn this and learn it well, and writing notes by hand was her best chance at retaining the information. Pearla asked Eric if he wouldn't mind being filmed as he reviewed the ins and outs of the security system, explaining she learned best by example and visuals. Eric was a patient instructor and a good sport.

"Whatever makes it easier."

With a sequence of mouse clicks, he brought up the video camera views. Five small squares filled the screen, labeled Living Room, Front Entrance, Pool Area, Courtyard, and Reception.

"These are the points the security cameras are trained on," he said. "The exterior are wide angle. Is there a time frame you want to see?"

"Let's look at the living room camera from 4:30 on Sunday afternoon. And if I remember correctly, we can speed it up and watch it continuously, right?"

"Yes, that's right. Here I'll show you." He proceeded to explain the steps and demonstrate how to move the cursor to speed up, slow down, or freeze frame an image to capture it and zoom in. Even though the film was black and white and rather grainy, it was possible to identify individual guests and themselves as they entered and exited the living room. The women watched as Rose McMartin looked furtively around before pocketing a wine glass and corkscrew and proceeding through the private door to the pantry kitchen.

Next, they watched the footage from the camera positioned under the eaves at the front of the inn. They saw the ambulance pull up, followed closely by the sheriff. The paramedics disappeared off screen as they rounded the corner at the front of the inn, heading toward the basement door. Sheriff Silva walked up the front steps before he went off screen.

"Switch to the reception camera," Pearla said. Eric clicked the drop-down menu and switched cameras. Now they saw the sheriff enter reception and stand at the front desk. Pearla greeted him and they quickly moved off-screen again.

"That's when I led him through the kitchen and down to the basement, but we don't have any cameras in those areas," Pearla lamented. Later footage showed Rose being wheeled out on a gurney and into the waiting ambulance, with Walt joining her. Even with the gaps, Max felt certain there was something the cameras must have caught that could help them figure out who hurt Rose McMartin. Not wanting to over-explain or reveal the reason they needed to access the footage, Max asked the questions necessary for her to grasp how the cameras worked.

"Thanks for all your help, Eric. We'll be in touch if we need more assistance with the cameras or the timers for the pool and exterior lights."

"No problem. Glad I could assist," Eric said.

When he left the office, Max turned to Pearla, "We need to inspect this more closely, now that we know what we're doing."

"I was thinking the exact same thing. When we installed these, I thought we were going overboard. Now I wish there were a few more so we could get a fuller picture of what happened. Let's look at all of Sunday, on all the cameras. I think that's the best place to start. We can speed it up and stop and go back if anything catches our eye." It was time for Pearla to clear away the breakfast set-up, so Max stayed to watch the film on her own.

"I'll text, or come get you if I see anything."

"Fingers crossed," Pearla said, and went to clean up after breakfast.

Max settled in, her glasses designed specifically for computer work balanced on her nose. She had all the camera angles visible in small squares on the screen. It helped that each camera location was labeled with the date and time in white under the image. If she stopped them, they were date and time stamped on the freeze frame. She clicked on the camera aimed at the front of the inn. They'd already watched as the ambulance then the sheriff pulled up and as they drove away. She backed up the video to watch again and calculate how much time the ambulance had spent parked out front before leaving.

She slowed down the video, then paused as a figure caught her eye. Barely visible, she could just make out a figure in the background, slipping behind the hedge of ficus trees lining the circular driveway in front of the inn. She froze the screen and zoomed in. The image was grainy. It was impossible to know whether she was looking at a male or female. The person had on pants and a dark sweatshirt and what looked like a beanie, or was that a short haircut? Too far away to tell. *Darn it*. But who was it, Max wondered.

After watching video footage from Sunday morning through evening, Max was no more enlightened about Rose's injury or accident or attempted murder. The only unusual thing she'd seen was the figure slipping behind the bushes before the ambulance pulled away. The other cameras had recorded only the guests moving about the grounds. It didn't help that Max wasn't sure what she was even looking for. It would take hours to try to re-create timelines for each of the guests, where they were and when, and there would be too many gaps with the cameras only able to capture certain angles. Without a camera trained on the cellar, she was no closer to answers. Then a thought occurred to her. Sheriff Silva had interviewed all the guests. He could review the footage to prove if they were telling the truth about their whereabouts. She would ask him when he stopped by later.

Chapter 32

Pearla

Pearla balanced a covered tray containing a plate with unseasoned scrambled eggs, dry toast, and a small dish of applesauce. A bag over her shoulder held a bottle of white grape juice. Setting the tray on the flagstone, Pearla used her spare key to unlock the front door of Max's cottage. She went straight to Char's room to find Max sitting on the bed, along with Butters. Char was propped up with pillows. When Pearla came in Char said, "This is so embarrassing. I feel like some kind of invalid."

"Nonsense," Pearla said. "Let me help. I brought all the things that always sure-fire make me feel better when my stomach's upset." She laid out the food on a lap tray Max had brought in.

"I tried to get up, but my head's so fuzzy," Char admitted. "I need to take my meds though. I'm glad you brought food. I think I can handle this."

"Where are your pills? Can I get them for you?" Pearla asked.

"On the bathroom counter," Char pointed to the en suite bathroom. "There are three bottles."

Pearla fetched the bottles and handed them over. "I'll start a pot of coffee. How does that sound?"

"Heavenly. I meant to get up earlier and brew a pot. I'm starting to feel less woozy," Char said after swallowing a bite of eggs. "Did Max tell you Parker proposed to Krista? It's the reason I had the champagne that wholly disagreed with me."

"No, she didn't." Pearla paused before adding, "Is that a good thing? What do you think? I don't mean to sound negative or anything, but it seems soon." Char took another bite of the eggs and followed it with a sip of juice.

"Actually, I'm glad you asked. I had the same concern. Just that it feels rushed. And out of the blue. He's wanting to arrange it right away. I haven't spoken to Krista privately, and I would never presume to discourage her. It's her decision, but if she's hesitant at all, I'm going to encourage her to take her time and not rush in. I'll suggest a long engagement."

"Good idea. I think she'll know you're just looking out for her." Pearla noticed the color was coming back into Char's delicate complexion. "You're looking better already," she remarked.

"Maybe I just needed something in my stomach. I think I'll rest and let this breakfast settle, then try to take a shower. Hey, can you hand me my laptop? It's over on the dresser."

"Sure. I'll pop back in later."

"Yes, I want to hear what the sheriff has to say. Max told me he was coming by." Pearla checked her phone and said, "He's due at eleven."

Charlene opened her laptop. No charge. She'd forgotten to plug it in.

Chapter 33

Sheriff Silva

Rene Silva knew this day would be a busy one, no sitting back in his office chair playing online chess or solitaire. He planned to get answers and put the collective mind of Silvermist Point at ease. As much as he'd like to keep the news of Beth's non-accidental death away from the public, it wasn't going to happen, and if he could craft the narrative, all the better. First stop, his office, where he would let slip to Janice that Beth's death was suspicious. She would spin it into her paper and he'd get information as people called in with tips. *Someone knows something.*

At 7:30 he arrived to find Larry Trawl waiting for him, holding a coffee from Front Porch and shifting from foot to foot anxiously. Janice was behind the counter of the mail desk looking busy, as was her specialty.

"Good morning, Larry. What brings you here so early?" he asked casually.

"I need to speak with you," the elder Trawl said.

"Come into my office," Rene invited and gestured to a plastic chair. He left the door open a crack. Larry set his coffee cup on the floor and wrung his hands in his lap, while Rene sensed a confession coming on.

"Take your time," he said, but made a point of looking at the clock on the wall and then at his watch. *Patience.* The floodgates opened and Larry's words poured out in a rush, while Rene scrambled to grab a pen and paper and take notes, not wanting to rely solely on his memory. *This is too important. I need to get it right.*

"Colby's not a bad kid."

Here we go. Confession time. Hold your tongue. Rene forced himself to listen attentively, nodding his head while offering minimal comments.

"I should have come to you sooner, like yesterday, but Beth's death has me so upset, and then seeing her body…"

"Go on," Rene encouraged.

Larry spoke on, describing how Colby saw Walt in Miscellaneous Goods and how he bluffed to Beth and saw the look of guilt on Walt's face, and how he saw Walt with Roxanne in the car. Rene took a full breath and waited for a beat before responding.

"So, do you think that's enough evidence to accuse Walt McMartin of murder? Your son is not the most reliable source, you know. Why should I trust him?"

"I knew you would say that." He leaned in conspiratorially. "Look, I could've kept this information to myself, but I'm an honest man. Also, there's one more thing. Colby found Beth's phone this morning in the trash at the inn, no sim card. Removed. He texted me a picture. It's hers. So, obviously Walt threw it away after murdering her."

"Um, that's quite a big leap. Who's to say Colby didn't murder her and is concocting this story to save his own butt?"

Larry was getting flustered and blurted rapidly. "Colby doesn't need a story. He didn't do it. Trust me. Plus, why would he knock out the old lady at the inn? He doesn't even know her. He never wants to see the inside of a jail again. He was drunk at Barnaby's the entire night. You can easily confirm that." Larry stopped speaking and was wheezing audibly. Rene sighed, then stood, holding out his hand.

"Thank you for stopping in. I'll follow up on that lead today, Mr. Trawl. Just make sure Colby is at the inn today. I'll need to get his statement."

Larry's face reddened and he stood up shakily and shook the sheriff's hand. "Alright then, I suppose that's all." He picked up his coffee and left the office.

Sheriff Silva grabbed his notepad and walked out soon after. He planned to visit Rose McMartin at the hospital before keeping his appointment with Pearla and Maxine at the inn at eleven. He finally felt as if he was getting somewhere with the case and that, if lucky, he could have it wrapped up by dinnertime.

* * *

Rene flashed his badge at the nurses' station as he asked in which room he could find Mrs. Rose McMartin. The nurse led him in and he saw Mrs. McMartin was sitting on the hospital bed, but dressed in regular clothing, except for her shoes. She had on those blue non-skid hospital socks. Hospital staff had issued Rene an identical pair when he had emergency surgery to remove his appendix a few years prior. He still sometimes wore them in the privacy of his cabin.

"She's waiting on her official release papers, as soon as the doctor clears her to go," the nurse explained, then addressed Mrs. McMartin.

"Mrs. McMartin, this is Sheriff Silva. He has a few questions, if that's okay." A young woman stood from a small sofa next to the bed and introduced herself.

"I'm Rose's daughter, Bella. What is this regarding, Sheriff? Is it about my mom's accident at the inn? She's still quite unclear about what happened."

"Well, yes. I'd like to ask her what she remembers about Sunday night." He watched Rose's expression change to something of relief.

"I've been wanting to talk to an authority, but no one believes me. I think my so-called friend tried to murder me. She was throwing herself at my husband. She's always been a flirt around men, but lately it's gotten out of hand and my husband enjoys the attention." She turned to her daughter. "I'm sorry to speak poorly of Daddy, but he was flirting right back, like some kind of lovesick teenager. I think they may have something going on, right under my nose. I don't trust them. I don't remember all of what happened on Sunday, but I remember wanting to drown my sorrows because I realized my husband and friend were having an affair."

It was a lot to process, but made sense to the sheriff. The puzzle was coming together in his mind. An affair was as good a motive as any. *Seems Larry Trawl was onto something.*

He was confident the ladies at the inn would provide more corroborating evidence, and Colby too, if he would talk. All that should be a reason to bring in Walt McMartin and his girlfriend, Roxanne, for questioning.

"What is your plan after your mother's released from the hospital?" he asked Bella.

"Well, I wanted to stay at the inn tonight, then head home tomorrow. I'm not sure what to do now. Mom seems convinced that Dad and Roxanne have it out for her."

"They do. I'm sure of it. That Roxanne has gotten into Walt's head. I told her about my pension too. I thought she was my friend. If I pass before Walt, he gets one hundred percent of my benefits. They could live large on that."

Bingo.

Tears fell, making her fresh makeup run. "You have to believe me. I'm not crazy."

He heard the panicked and frantic edge in her voice. Sheriff Silva was not the best at comforting people, but he reached out and touched the woman's arm reassuringly.

"Don't worry. We'll sort this all out. I'm on my way to the inn, and I plan to get to the bottom of what happened Sunday night."

"Do you think it'll be safe for us to stay there tonight? I don't know if we can find other accommodations," Bella remarked.

"You'll be perfectly safe at the inn." In his mind, Rene saw the afternoon play out. He would roll up to the inn and leave with Walt and Roxanne in the back of his patrol car, no siren, too dramatic. They'd arrive at Brookhaven station for questioning. He would elicit a confession, level the charge, and make the arrest. *There's no honor among thieves. One of them will rat out the other once I question them alone.*

Chapter 34

Krista

For a woman whose routine was utterly predictable, *okay, boring,* these last few days had provided more new experiences and excitement than Krista's entire adult life up to this point. To stay at this magical place, to meet a cousin she never knew she had, and to finally, *finally* have a man love her and actually want to marry her, was surreal. Krista wanted to keep pinching herself and reminding herself with positive affirmations, that she deserved this. She was worthy.

Parker tapped at her door with his usual three short knocks, and she sprang out of bed and welcomed him. He was dressed in a t-shirt and running shorts and smelled of fresh soap. His hair was damp and pulled into a loose ponytail. It was a different look than his usual boho grunge style, and she did not dislike it. He kissed her lightly and pulled her close, cuddling her. Still, he was ever the gentleman, and asked while nuzzling her neck and planting light kisses, "So have you given any more thought to my proposal?" He pulled her next to him to sit on the edge of the bed. Krista wasn't capable of playing it cool. She only knew how to be forthright and speak honestly. She looked deep into his eyes.

"Parker, I've been in love with you since our first date." She felt a rush through her whole body saying the words out loud. "I want nothing more than to be your wife, but I'd be sad without having my dad present and at least a few friends." Krista longed to shop for and choose the perfect white dress. She wanted a church wedding and flowers and a small reception and an unforgettable honeymoon in some exotic place. Of course she would never voice these desires aloud to Parker. She didn't want to come across as demanding. A small part of her was still reeling in disbelief that he could really love her. She didn't want to push her luck.

"Wouldn't you want your friends and family there too?" she asked hopefully. *On the most special day of our lives.*

"I guess I wasn't thinking about it. I'm not close with my family, but yeah, I suppose they should be there."

Krista dreaded sounding desperate, but had to ask, "Do they know about me? Don't they want to meet me?"

"Look, don't take this the wrong way," he smoothed her hair. "But they do their own thing. I rarely see them. We aren't close. Eventually they'd meet you. Besides, you have your dad. And Char. She's amazing. I can't believe how much we have in common, all the places we've both been."

"Right. I hope we'll be able to travel someday too," Krista said, wistfully. It was yet another thing that made her feel out of place. She'd never left the country and had only been to three states as a kid.

"We will. Look, I haven't been completely honest with you. I've dated a lot of women who were only after me for my money."

"What money? You only have your job and a small allowance, right?"

"Not exactly."

Krista wasn't sure what to expect, but sat silently waiting. Parker tugged on his ponytail and seemed fidgety.

"I'll never have to work a day in my life if I don't want to; neither will you. We can travel whenever we want. To wherever you want."

"What are you saying? I don't understand. Parker, I enjoy my job. I've worked hard to get where I am. I don't love you for your money. I'm not like that."

"I know. And that's why I love you." *He said it! Don't react too much.*

"I love you too," she said, enjoying the taste of the words.

"Hey, have you heard from Char this morning?" Parker asked, his voice laced with concern. Krista remembered then how they had left Char at the hot tub.

"I hope she's feeling okay. I was worried about her after we left last night."

"She sure can knock back the drinks." Parker scratched his neck and pulled at the collar of his shirt.

"What? Like is she an alcoholic? Is that what you're thinking?"

"I don't know. I mean, you don't really know her. People can hide it well. I should know. I come from a long line of alcoholics. That's why I'm so careful."

Krista didn't like the insinuation that Char had a problem, but who was she to say? Maybe Char did. Lots of people have issues with alcohol. Parker sneezed and rubbed his eyes. "I hope you're not getting a cold," Krista said.

"No, I think I'm allergic to something. I just started having a reaction in your room. I usually only react like this to cats. I'm highly allergic." Butters had been a regular visitor to Krista's room.

"Oh no, it's Butters, Max's cream tabby. I've let him in here. He's such a cutie."

"Yup, that's what's causing the reaction," Parker confirmed.

Krista felt bad, but there was no way she could have known. Butters was so sweet she couldn't help but spoil him. She'd always wanted her own cat and was thinking of adopting one. *Maybe a dog instead. I hope he's not allergic to dogs, too.* Parker stood.

"Well, I'm going for a run. I've been up a while, already had some breakfast, and a coffee. Are you gonna get up soon, sleepyhead?"

"Yes, I need some coffee. Come find me when you get back."

He kissed her on the cheek and left. Krista was surprised when she realized it was after ten. She was finally allowing herself to relax. It would not be easy going back to work on Monday. The entire week had seemed like a dream, and she didn't want reality to spoil it.

She glanced at her ring finger, imagining a beautiful engagement ring there. *He loves me.* Yes, she wanted more than a rushed wedding. She'd waited her whole life for this, a little longer would be worth it. Parker had suggested the cliffside, but Krista longed for a church wedding or at least a minister to preside, and a reception on the Snowy Plover Inn grounds. She would find Max and Pearla and ask if that was a possibility.

Chapter 35

Maxine

When the sheriff finally rolled up after one, not at eleven as expected, relief coursed through Max's body. She didn't have supreme confidence in him, not even close, but she figured if he'd hear them out, they could work together to solve what happened to Beth and Rose and clear the way for a far less dramatic second week at the inn. Silvermist Point was a tiny town and the sooner she could drive the cloud of suspicion away from the inn, the better.

"Sheriff, we're so glad you're here. We have some information to share that we believe will help with the investigation. We didn't want to interfere, but we're in a unique position here and we've observed our guests and, well..." Pearla chimed in.

"Hi there, Sheriff." *She's flirting.* Max smirked.

"I'm a bit of a mystery buff, and I couldn't help but look at the evidence. I really think we might be useful to the investigation. Can we step into the office where there's more privacy? And video camera footage." *That oughta get his attention.* Once they were in the office, Max showed him the camera angles on the computer screen.

"You can use this to verify all the guests' whereabouts from Sunday evening," Pearla explained. "You know, make sure they were where they said they were, that their stories check out."

"Well, well. That's impressive ladies. Been doing a little spy work, have you?" he said with a chuckle.

Is this man laughing at us?

"Don't get me wrong, while I certainly appreciate your help, I've got this matter all tied up. Are Walt McMartin and Roxanne Whitam on the grounds?" Max glanced at Pearla who raised an eyebrow.

"Yes. I believe so. Both of their cars are in the lot."

"I'll need to speak with them. I plan to take them down to the main station in Brookhaven for questioning."

Interesting. Play it cool.

"What's making you lean in that direction?" Max asked. "Because we have some information on another guest that seems incriminating. We wanted to share our findings with you."

Sheriff Silva scratched his beard, then asked, "What do you all think about Colby Trawl?"

"He's shady," Pearla blurted. "Also, we found receipts from Miscellaneous Goods in the golf cart."

"That he took without permission," Max added.

"On the night of Beth's disappearance." Pearla looked

expectantly at Rene Silva.

"But we're even more suspicious of the writer."

Rene Silva's eyes popped at this and a small smile played at the corners of his mouth.

"The writer? Why?"

Pearla explained how Ms. Singer had been married twice and both husbands died under suspicious circumstances. The professor found searches for disposing of a body on her computer, and calls herself a method writer who happens to be switching from romance to crime.

"When you say it out loud, it sounds outlandish," Max admitted.

"Maybe a little," Rene said. "I appreciate you keeping me in the loop, ladies. But you should know, I'm confident I have the perp. As soon as it's official and he, or they, are booked, I'll share more details." He paused thoughtfully before adding, "Maybe give Colby a break. He was helpful on this. Have him call me, will you? You have my number."

Max led the sheriff out to the pool where they found Walt and Roxanne sitting next to each other on loungers looking like they hadn't a care in the world.

He's about to rock their world.

Walt was surly, and said, "You've got to be kidding me. This is a mistake," but he was cooperative.

Roxanne was not. Shouting insults and saying he would hear from her lawyer and she wasn't gonna say one thing down at the station.

"Just do what he says," Walt advised. "We know we're innocent. Just shut up and calm down."

Before driving off, Rene came back to the front steps where Pearla and Max stood watching the scene, as Rene locked the pair in the back of the police car.

"Thanks for keeping us safe," Pearla said.

"It's my pleasure. All in a day's work. I should warn you," he said, glancing skyward. "The fog is supposed to roll in this afternoon. Not sure if you've experienced it yet. It's quite something. You're best to stay put, your guests too. If anyone is planning to leave the area, they should get on the road now."

"I remember the fog," Max said. "But we haven't had it since I've been back. Never seen anything like it since." She turned to Pearla. "You're gonna love it, it's so otherworldly."

"Thanks again, Sheriff."

"Call me Rene."

"Okay. Thanks for your help, Rene," Pearla grinned.

"I'll be in touch." And with that he rolled out with Walt and Roxanne arguing in the back of the patrol car.

"I wonder what they're saying?" Pearla said.

"I think we can guess," Max replied.

By then, all the occupants of the inn had heard the commotion and watched as Walt and Roxanne were driven away. Later, when Rose and her daughter Bella showed up, Max led them into the living room for some refreshments and she gently broke the news that Walt and Roxanne had been taken into custody.

"Well, that's a relief," Rose said. "I don't know what to believe anymore, but if the sheriff brought them in for questioning, then I know I'm not completely off-base."

"Oh Mom, we'll get it sorted. For now, let's just relax."

Good daughter, trying to keep her mom calm.

"I'm sorry I missed the whole week here and had to spend it in the hospital." Rose's voice was sad, her disappointment obvious.

"Well, we'll just have to come back. It'll be a mother-daughter, girls-only retreat." Max felt the love Bella had for her mother.

"I'd love that, Bella. Let's book it for next month. It's so charming here."

"We would love to have you back," Max encouraged. The women each loaded a plate with delicacies from the charcuterie board.

"I think I'll have a glass of wine," Rose said.

"One should be okay. I'll pour, and we can take it to our rooms," Bella replied.

"I'll carry over your luggage," Max said. It was nearing six and the fog was rapidly rolling in. "I'm glad you beat the fog."

Chapter 36

Charlene

As she sat in the office swivel chair, Charlene couldn't take her eyes off the monitor. She was feeling marginally better and had offered to review the camera footage. She hoped to spot something useful that she could relay to the sheriff when he arrived. So far, nothing struck her as out-of-the-ordinary. She already knew Walt and Roxanne had been in and out of each other's rooms as had the professor and Ms. Singer. After he shared his suspicions with Pearla, Keith Lombard had apparently avoided the writer. At least they weren't seen together again on the monitor screen. The views were frustratingly limited to only where the cameras were, and as such, couldn't catch everything.

Charlene wanted to look at last night's footage, but was

so far, avoiding it. *So embarrassing.* Finally, she clicked on the pool and hot tub view. In real time, Roxanne and Walt were sitting on loungers. She, reading a book and he, scrolling on his phone. Char backed it up to the previous night. She watched Parker pour champagne and saw the three of them raise their glasses in a toast. She sped forward and observed herself exit the hot tub to turn the bubbles back on. *Was I wobbly?* She watched as Parker poured her a second glass. Sure enough, she drank it. Two glasses wouldn't normally cause this kind of reaction and brutal hangover.

Five minutes forward and Krista and Parker got out of the hot tub. Parker reached down and topped off Char's glass. *That must have been the tipping point.* They left after that and Char stayed. She watched her head bob up and down as if she was struggling to stay awake. She rested her head on the edge of the tub and appeared to be sleeping. Charlene shivered. *What if I'd gone under? I might have drowned.* Then Maxine came onto the screen and Char saw herself lifted out by her armpits. She struggled to stand, leaning on Max. Then staggered and vomited in the bushes. It was morbidly embarrassing, but she didn't look away.

After she and Max had left, she continued to stare at the screen. Moths flitted by and steam rose from the hot tub and the pool in the cool night air. It was so peaceful. She was about to click the cameras back to real time and leave the office when Parker came on screen. He walked past the pool and over to the hot tub. *He came to check on me. How thoughtful.* He bent down and picked up something. The wineglass she'd left behind. Charlene was relieved that it had been Max to rescue her. She wasn't sure she could bear the shame of being lifted up, too out of it to stand, and getting sick in front of her cousin's boyfriend.

Chapter 37

Pearla

"This type of fog is called advection fog. It's common on the California coastline when warm moist air passes over a colder surface," Keith Lombard explained. "I enjoy it, but I don't think I would if I experienced it too often. It's dangerous and best to stay put until it clears. It's easy to lose your way in it. There are always accidents when it rolls in, especially with people not accustomed to it."

Ms. Singer appeared suddenly, like an apparition, at the living room doors off the patio. She came in with the fog clawing at her heels and closed the door swiftly to trap it outside. Bundled up in a throw blanket, she lugged her large handbag tucked under her arm.

"This fog is incredible, so atmospheric! Can I grab a

cup of tea? I'm headed up to the tower to get some writing in."

"I'd like to see the view from up there," Keith remarked.

"Well, you know you're welcome to join me. I don't own it," the writer said pointedly, then smirking, added, "unless you still think I'm dangerous."

Ouch.

"I didn't expect it to move in this quickly. I can barely see two feet in front of me," Pearla said to break the tension as she lit the fireplace in the living room.

"Tyne called. He said to have lanterns and candles at the ready. He reminded me we don't have a generator here," Max said.

"Why would we need candles? To make it more eerie than it already is?" Pearla asked.

"No. He said we're likely to lose power here. The old conductors often spark and go out with this type of fog. They haven't been updated. Tyne's got a generator at Barnaby's, but he plans to close early. He says folks tend to stay home with fog this thick."

"What are the guests going to do about dinner if they aren't supposed to drive anywhere and Barnaby's is closing early?"

"Well, there's just a few of us. I can cook something up and we can eat family style in the living room. The sheriff said not to drive. I'd feel better if everyone stayed here. We don't need an accident or a guest getting lost."

Bella and Rose came in via the back patio, followed by Krista and Parker.

"I'm glad we found our way back," Krista said, pushing back her damp hair. "We were out on the shore when we saw the fog moving toward us. We were way down the coast, at least a mile away."

"It felt like we were being chased by it. Like it's alive," Parker added dramatically.

"And it got so dark, so quick," Bella said and turned to Rose. "Mom, I'm glad we didn't keep driving."

"Me too. We're safe here."

Pearla noted the emphasis Rose put on the word 'safe'. The guests gathered in the living room and listened to the conductor spark, a brief warning before the lights flicked and the power was lost. They were momentarily plunged into semi-darkness, before Pearla turned on a battery lantern and Max lit some candles.

"Well, I guess I'm not cooking. Even if the stove's gas, I can't see well enough to do a great job." Pearla could hear Max's effort to keep a lighthearted tone.

"Let's see what all the guests would like and we'll call in an order to Tyne before the restaurant closes. He can have someone drop it by. It's a short distance. Should be fine."

Pearla found a copy of the menu, and the guests passed it around choosing their entrees. Everyone was in good spirits, considering.

"I've got puzzles and games in the cabinets," Max offered. "With the fireplace and lanterns, the light's okay in here." Then to Pearla, "I should go check on Char. She fell asleep again. I don't want her to wake up in darkness with the lights not working."

"We had tea with her before we went for a walk," Krista said.

"She seemed fine then," Parker said. "Must've been a stomach bug."

Pearla chose an old candle lantern and went upstairs. She didn't want to deplete her phone battery. Something did not feel right. She knew logically there was nothing to fear, but her heart felt strained and her body buzzed with a low-level panic. *I'm being paranoid. I've never liked the dark.* This wasn't altogether true. Pearla didn't mind darkness and even preferred it while she slept, no nightlight for her. So what was it? She reasoned it was more the feeling of a loss of control. It was a different matter when you chose the darkness, but when it came unbidden and there was nothing you could do about it, it felt threatening.

She checked her phone battery and noticed it was fifty percent. She would put in a quick call to Rene. He could relay what went on at the station with Walt and Roxanne. Talking to him, she felt, could stem her panic knowing she needn't worry about a guest with murderous inclinations.

Can we talk? She sent the text and waited for his response. Two minutes later her phone rang.

"Hi, Pearla. How can I help you?" Rene's voice was confident. Pearla felt better already. *He must have saved me as a contact.*

"Just wondering if you could share what's happening with Walt and Roxanne." *How shall I phrase this?* "What I mean to say is, are we sure they're responsible for Rose's injury and Beth's death?"

"I'm certain enough to have brought them in. After all, they're the only ones with an obvious motive. I can't share details quite yet, but trust me. We have enough to hold them tonight, so you're safe in that regard."

"I do trust you. It's not that. I just can't shake this awful feeling that there's more to it. Call it intuition. It's not helping that we lost power and the fog's so thick we're essentially trapped here. I guess I just want assurance that we're safe."

"The fog's not so bad here at the station in Brookhaven, but I hear in Silvermist, it's next level. No one's going anywhere tonight. Listen, I'm planning to stay here and not drive in till morning after it clears. It's dangerous out there."

"That makes sense. I guess that's all then. Thanks for talking with me. I better preserve my phone battery. We still have one hard wired landline here, so I'll use that if I need to call again."

"Well, don't hesitate."

Pearla sensed he might want to say more; it was so hard to read intent over the phone.

"I appreciate that," Pearla said. And she did. It was comforting that he was a phone call away, but unsettling that it would take him at least forty-five minutes to drive here in the fog, and that's if he was willing. Pearla glanced at her cell battery, now down to thirty-five percent. The only landline was an old black rotary phone in reception. The other inn phones they'd replaced with cordless, and those needed power to function.

Back in the living room, she finalized the guests' orders, then called into Barnaby's. Tyne said he'd have it delivered within the hour.

Chapter 38

Charlene

When Krista and Parker came by the cottage, Charlene was feeling better, but wondered how out of it she had seemed to them the night before. *So embarrassing.*

"Terrible stomach bug," she explained. "It hit me out of nowhere."

"Glad you're feeling better," Parker said and poured her some tea. They chatted about kayaking and snorkeling in the waters off the California Channel Islands.

"You've got to experience it, Kris, I'll take you," Parker said.

What an attentive and loving man. We should all be so lucky.

Char thanked them for stopping by and said she'd see them later. "I'm gonna take it easy."

She was thrilled for her cousin, but nevertheless, she planned to look into Parker's past. She had learned how to follow online leads to gain access to people's profiles and personal information, all of which was available to the public on the web, but you needed to know how to search for it and most people didn't. Plus, people who wanted to hide stuff could be very savvy at doing so, so you needed practice if you wanted to really look into someone. She'd learned this the hard way.

Char knew she should ask permission. Krista might perceive it as a violation of trust, but she was young and wouldn't understand the value and peace of mind a thorough examination into a potential partner's life could provide. The thought probably never crossed her mind. *She doesn't need to know.*

This was something Char could do behind the scenes. Parker gave her no reason to be suspicious, but neither had any of the soul-sucking louses she had dated. It was just a layer of protection, and Krista would never even know she'd done it unless there was a reason to be concerned.

Char returned to her room and opened her laptop, now charged with a full battery. She typed **Parker Graves** into a general search first. Lots of matches, but no images that looked like him, and she didn't know if he had a middle name. *Hmm.* She tried by location, but no one matched. The ones she found were too old or the image was wrong. Nothing on social media either. It was possible he kept a low profile, or maybe went by his middle name instead of his given name. Char felt her head begin to spin, and she was hit by a wave of nausea. *I really must have the flu. I need to call my doctor.* She leaned back on the pillows and fell asleep.

* * *

"Char, are you up?" Max tiptoed in whispering. "We lost power. I brought you a battery lantern."

Char's words came out in a flurry. "I must have fallen asleep again, or passed out. I really am sick, I guess. My head's spinning. Did you say we lost power?" She sat up feeling disoriented. "What time is it?"

Max joined her on the bed. "A little after seven. Tyne warned me earlier we might lose power. There's ridiculously thick fog. You've got to see it. Remember when we used to walk around in it years ago? It's just like that, so thick you can't see two feet in front of you."

"I want to get up, but I'm so tired, and dizzy again."

Max walked over to the large windows and pulled the curtains all the way open. "You can kind of see it from here, but it mostly looks dark."

"How are the guests doing? Are they freaking out without power? Thank God, Roxanne's not here. I can hear her whining about the inconvenience. Not to mention she and Walt might be murderers. There's that too," Char said, unable to keep herself from chuckling. "What a first week, right? Trial by fire."

"More like trial by murder and fog," Max said. "That sounds like a good book title. Maybe Ms. Singer would like the suggestion."

Char laughed again.

"The guests are in the living room. We found a menu from Barnaby's and called in an order for everyone. Tyne had one of his employees bring it over. I got extra soup, garden salads, and a couple club sandwiches. I wasn't sure what you'd feel like eating and I wanted leftovers."

"Thanks, Max. This is one of the many reasons you're my best friend," Char felt tears spring up and she reached to hug Max. "I'll wash my face and get up. Where are Krista and Parker?"

"They were in the living room, but they took their food upstairs."

Char confessed to Max that she'd tried to research Parker's background on the web.

"Did you find anything?"

"No. That's the strange part. Nothing at all. Literally nothing. That's weird, right?"

"I don't know. Seems like there'd be basic stuff. Address, places of work, relatives, images. I couldn't find anything, not even social media profiles. I wonder if he has a different name, or paid to have his presence scrubbed. Maybe that's it. Krista did mention he was very private. I use a different name online. Very few people know my real name, so maybe it's the same for him."

"That would make sense. You could ask Krista what she knows. There has to be a way without sounding too nosy. Let's think about it."

Char's cell chirped and she picked it up off the nightstand. "It's Krista," she whispered to Max as she answered it. "I'm fine, thanks. I got woozy again and fell asleep after you and Parker left. How was the walk on the beach?" Charlene looked thoughtful as she listened. "What, really? That's great." Char leaned over and whispered to Max, "He gave her a ring."

"Well, that's good," Max said.

"She's sending a photo," Char said while covering the mic. "Hey, can I put you on speaker? I'm here with Max."

"Of course. I probably shouldn't be wearing out my battery, but I didn't want to come over and wake you if you were sleeping. I was just gonna send the photo. I wanted you to see it, get your reaction. It was his great grandmother's. A family heirloom, so he must have been planning to ask me all along."

"I don't see it yet," Char peered at her phone.

"The reception's bad here. It may not come through, but you can show us in person," Max said.

"I'll come down. I wanted to ask you about having the wedding and reception at the inn. I can't think of a more perfect place."

"I'd be honored to have it here," Max gushed and smiled at Char.

"I'll come over to the cottage in a few minutes." Krista hung up. Char looked at her phone again and saw the picture come up.

"Here it is." She held the phone between herself and Max and they leaned in to see the image as Char zoomed in.

"That's so dainty and pretty," Max remarked.

Char looked closer, then zoomed more. "Wow."

Krista joined them in the cottage and showed them the ring up close.

"It's so much like the one you admired in the shop," Char said.

"I was thinking the same. I'm taking it as a sign. It's a family heirloom. It must be from the same time period, maybe even the same designer. He knows pink is my favorite color," Krista said.

"Where is he now?" Char asked.

"He said he'd be down soon. He was going to try to make some calls if he can get a signal. I think he's telling his parents he asked me to marry him. I hope they'll come to the wedding. I haven't met them yet. They've been in

England. I'll finally get to meet his roommates too. It's all so much. Everything I've prayed for."

I hope so. You deserve a man who will treat you right.

Chapter 39

Maxine

M s. Singer had set herself up in a plush side chair and was using a small table as a makeshift writing desk. The author was writing by hand in a leather notebook depending on candlelight and the warm glow of the stone fireplace. *In that black hoodie, she could be mistaken for a man.* Max's mind went to the video footage she'd seen earlier.

"Tell me more about your writing process, Ms. Singer. Do you have a certain word count goal each day, or do you write as inspiration strikes?"

"Mmm, it depends." She was quick to answer, but clearly wanted to get back to her writing and not become immersed in conversation.

Max noted that Keith Lombard was keeping a respectable distance from the writer, but Max imagined his ears perking up at the conversation. He had expressed his opinion to her earlier, confiding, "I know the sheriff made his arrest, but I'm telling you, I still feel like I don't trust that woman. There's just something about her energy." Max hadn't known how to respond. She, like Pearla, was relieved at the arrests of Walt and Roxanne, but still felt unsettled.

I blame the fog.

Keith Lombard was the only guest Pearla had not outright suspected. Was it possible she'd overlooked him? What about Colby? He seemed like a bumbling idiot half the time, but he definitely bore a grudge, and was no fan of Beth. Sheriff Rene promised he'd clear it all up and answer questions, but he hadn't yet. And now they were plunged into darkness. The feeling that Walt and Roxanne were not the guilty ones continued to plague her, but why?

The patio door swung open and Colby unceremoniously pushed his way inside the living room followed by his father. The men stood there looking soggy, disheveled, and stunned before Larry asked, "Is there anything you need? I realized you might not be prepared for a power outage. Can I help you find more lanterns? I just wanted to check in on you."

Wow!

"That was so thoughtful, Mr. Trawl." Max chose her words carefully. She still wasn't sure about the motives of these two.

"Tyne Barnaby warned me earlier there might be an outage. Pearla and I found the lanterns in the shed, enough to give each guest one. The fireplace is giving us some decent, low light in here and we located a bunch of candles too." In a rush of unexplained goodwill, she added, "Are you hungry? We ordered food from Barnaby's and I have leftovers at the cottage." Larry raised his eyebrows. He looked as surprised as Max felt.

"We'd like that. We don't have power in the trailer."

"Not much food, either," Colby added.

"It's settled then. Just have a seat, and I'll go make you some plates." Max hurried out followed by Pearla who whispered under her breath, "Why are we being so nice?"

"You know, keep your friends close and your enemies closer," Max said.

"True. I agree we need them in our corner. Besides, they didn't have to check on us. They're showing good will and we probably should too."

"Plus, I don't want to be on their bad side." The ladies made up two plates of food from Max's kitchen, covered them in foil and returned to the living room. Larry and Colby were sitting at one end of the large table. Krista and Charlene were chatting amiably with them and asking if there had been many weddings hosted at the inn. Parker appeared from the reception area, guided by the flashlight on his phone.

"I suppose you've all heard then?" Parker announced as he joined them. "About Krista and me getting married? The sooner the better."

Colby stood and scrutinized him. "Hey, I know you. We met at Barnaby's in town."

"No. I don't think so. Sorry, man."

"No, it's definitely you. Robert, right? We met Monday night. You were drunk as a skunk. No offense. I was too," Colby laughed raucously.

"He wasn't here Monday," Pearla said. "He just checked in Tuesday night." Max watched the scene play out. Colby shook his head back and forth.

"And his name's Parker," Char added.

"Yeah, Bro. Not me," Parker said and backed away. Colby didn't respond. Max watched as he clenched his fists. For a second, she thought he might bang them on the table like some kind of neanderthal caveman, but then he squeezed his eyes shut, opened them and focused on his plate. He stabbed a bite of salad and shoveled it into his mouth. Larry Trawl gave him an awkward pat on the back and whispered something in his ear that Max couldn't quite decipher. Tension hung in the air.

Please don't lose your cool.

"Parker, can I borrow your phone flashlight for a minute?" Pearla asked.

"Uh, actually, my battery's low. I should turn it off."

"Right. I'll use a lantern. Max, can you come with me? I think I can find some dessert for everyone. Maybe some cookies?" Max heard the panicked edge and a rushed quality in Pearla's words. She'd known her long enough to pick up on the subtlety. Max shot Char a glance and followed Pearla to the kitchen.

"Cookies would be great with this tea," Char said, taking a gulp. Max and Pearla went through the swinging door into the kitchen.

"Hurry. Get to the reception desk," Pearla urged. "We need to call the sheriff."

"He's too far away. In Brookhaven." Max wasn't sure what was happening, and she struggled to maintain her composure as a level of panic rose in her chest, squeezing her lungs.

"What's happening?" she whispered. Pearla tucked behind the desk and pulled Max down beside her.

"Don't think I'm losing it, please. I don't feel safe." She reached up and grabbed the hard-wired phone, picked up the receiver, and punched in 911. She held the receiver to her ear.

"This should work without power. That's why we kept the line." She held the receiver away from her ear. "I can't get a dial tone. It's dead." Max pulled the cord. It flopped down.

"Oh my gosh! It's cut!" Pearla croaked as she squeezed Max's arm tightly.

"If I wasn't freaking out before, I am now. I'm texting Tyne. You grab some cookies and go act normal," Max said. She took a deep breath. *Get control.* "You know we're probably worried for nothing." As she said the words, she desperately wished them to be true. Max crouched low behind the desk and turned on her phone. The red line warned of only 10% battery life. She typed quick and hit send, hoping her message would convey her desperation.

TYNE COME QUICK EMERGENCY & CALL 911!!!!!
What else can I do?

Max wasn't sure at this point who she should be afraid of, or if she and Pearla were overreacting. Fingers flying, she quickly sent a second text to let Tyne know they were in danger: **NOT SAFE. HELP** and hit send, but the little wheel just spun and refused to send. *I knew I should have replaced the battery.* Max watched helplessly as her phone went to 1%, then died. She hadn't memorized Tyne's number, so all she could do was hope he'd gotten the message and was still at work. If he was, he should be able to get here in ten minutes, but if he'd gone home ... Max didn't know how far away he lived from the village.

What if he doesn't get the message at all?

Chapter 40

Pearla

Ms. Singer cleared her throat, "Since you're all so curious about what I'm writing, it's a murder mystery."

Who said they were curious?

"Interesting," Pearla said, keeping her tone neutral.

"I've done some extensive research so I'm confident it will read as an authentic account, a dive into the mind of a killer, if you will. In the most popular thrillers, the killers are always men. Every book I read and movie I watch. We need more cold-blooded women who are the killers, that's what I think. I'm betting there's a market for it too. I wanted to set the story at an inn, so a lot of the details might ring very familiar. You might even find yourself characterized in the novel, but it's fictional of course. All names and likenesses have been altered and any resemblance to anyone alive, or dead, is strictly a coincidence."

"Is it written in the first person point of view?" Keith asked.

Pearla wanted to shoot him a mad dog stare, but it was too dark in the room. *Don't bait her.* She was counting the minutes until Tyne would arrive, praying Max's message went through. It was taking all the courage she could muster to act normal and serve cookies with a killer in the room. Bella stood and took her mother's arm.

"We'll be leaving now. Give us a minute, please, before you continue with your story. I don't think my mom needs to be subjected to this after all she's been through. I can't believe you'd take a tragedy and spin it into a book just to make money. So insensitive. Come on, Mom. Let's go," Bella said and led her mom away.

"Well, I see nothing wrong with what you're doing," Parker raised his voice. "She's a writer, folks. Gotta get ideas from somewhere. Besides, money's what makes the world go round. Those who don't have it, want it. And those of us who have it, always want more. Isn't that right, cousin Char?"

"Char?" When she didn't respond, Krista moved next to her on the small sofa and shook her gently.

"She's passed out." Krista's voice was full of concern as she attempted to rouse her cousin. She felt Char's forehead and checked her pulse.

"Pearla, we need an ambulance. I think something's wrong. She's not been well. Her breathing is too shallow. Parker, dial 911." Parker made no move to use his phone.

"Probably snuck a little nip into that tea. She can't hold

her alcohol. Does that run in your family, Krista? You'd better be careful."

"You're a jerk," Colby said. "And a liar too. You and me both know you were at that bar on Monday night. And you sure as heck shouldn't be calling anyone out about their drinking habits. What did you do when the bar closed? Where did you go? Cause now I think about it, I saw you in Beth's shop Monday, too."

"You are crazy, nothing but a crazy hillbilly. You all heard him. This man is nuts."

"No. You've got something to hide, is what I think." Colby lunged for him and grabbed hold of his shirt. Parker struck back with a punch to Colby's face. An audible crunch and Colby's nose began to spurt blood. Stunned, Colby covered his nose, blood dripping through his fingers.

"Calm down, gentlemen," Ms. Singer said, never flinching or moving from her chair. "Someone toss him some napkins. It'll be tough to get blood out of this area rug."

"Well, you should know," Keith said.

Is she enjoying this?

Then Pearla saw the glint of a blade in the dim light. Before she reacted, Parker plunged it into Colby's upper chest near his right shoulder. Colby fell backward in a heap, one hand still clutching his nose and the other his upper chest. He pulled his knees up and tucked his head in a fetal position, moaning like a wounded animal.

"Parker. Stop. What are you doing?" Krista shrieked.

"I'm protecting you. This man is a psychopath. Go upstairs and lock yourself in your room. I'll deal with this situation down here. I'll take care of Char and call an ambulance, I promise."

Confusion and hurt crossed Krista's features.

"Parker, whose phone is that?" she asked calmly.

"It's mine."

"No, it's not. I've never seen it before."

I have, in your luggage.

"Why are we talking about phones right now?"

Pearla understood that Krista was keeping Parker distracted. *At least I think that's what she's up to.*

Colby moaned on the floor.

"You, Bird Man. Help me get this guy tied up. We should tie up the old man, too."

"The hell you will," Larry said and wielded the fireplace poker. "I'll smash your skull in."

"Ladies, let the men handle this," Parker said, as if the men were grilling meat at a barbeque and they tasked the ladies with bringing them beers.

"I don't know what you're playing at, but it's not funny," Keith said. "You just stabbed someone! We need a first aid kit. This has gone too far."

"The writer can stay. She can put it in her book." Parker continued, "Matter of fact, I'm not sure she's a lady."

The room fell silent as everyone's attention focused on the sound of car tires crunching on gravel and the sight of headlights shining through the glass double doors of the reception foyer.

Pearla thought fast.

"Must be a guest who got stuck in the fog. They probably want to stop for the night. I'll just go and settle them in."

"You'll go nowhere," Parker said. "I have a gun, too. And I'll use it. Do what I say, and no one gets hurt. I didn't mean to stab the guy. He threatened me, you all witnessed it. Now, maybe I overreacted and I'm sorry about that. Krista and I will leave now. Krista, get your stuff."

No one moved or spoke. Everyone was rooted where they stood or sat.

"No, get in the car. Forget about your things. Just get in the car! Right now!" Parker's voice was frantic.

He's losing it. Don't do something stupid.

Krista broke the silence. "You're right, this is too much and I want to leave. I don't have my keys, honey; I'll go get them." Krista broke away and ran for the stairs calling, "I'll be right back."

Pearla knew the front door was locked. Tyne would need to walk around and enter through the patio doors.

"Oh, now I get it. I just put the pieces together. You little devil. Nice plan, Parker," Ms. Singer said, and began writing furiously in her notebook.

"You better stop talking," Parker said, his voice tinged with a murderous edge.

Chapter 41

Saturday
Max

S o what happened next?" Sawyer asked as Max rehashed the events from the previous night. She was still processing everything herself. In her wildest dreams she would not have been able to forecast a grand opening and first week like the one they had. Sawyer had surprised her by showing up at the inn. Char knew he was coming, but had kept the secret, which was very unusual for her.

Max, Char, Krista, Sawyer, and Pearla were together in Max's comfortable cottage, flopped on the two overstuffed sofas, Char in a recliner, with her slippered feet up. Butters was making up for lost time with Sawyer, head butting him and purring loudly as Sawyer brushed and petted him.

Max continued the story of what had gone down less than twenty-four hours prior.

"It all avalanched from there. Parker lunged at the author with the knife, but Colby straightened out his leg and tripped him. When Parker hit the floor, the author sprung out of her chair and delivered a sharp, perfectly placed kick, right in the family jewels." Max watched as Sawyer winced at the thought.

"Perfect. That jerk deserved it. Sorry, Mom. Please continue."

"Hmm, so next, Larry Trawl took the knife from Parker, then held him down with a foot on his back. He was basically incapacitated by the time Tyne arrived just minutes later."

"I'll bet! And he didn't have a gun? He was bluffing?"

"Yup, no gun. Tyne had one though." *Like some action hero come to life.* "He and Keith, that's the professor I told you about, zip-tied Parker's hands behind his back. Then, in some divine and perfect timing, the lights came on. It was quite dramatic, honestly."

"I missed all the drama. I was out cold at the time," Char said.

"The sheriff came later and searched Parker's room. Seems he was new to the murder game. The sheriff found searches on his phone and drugs in his bag," Max said.

"Turns out, he was drugging me. Slipping Valium into my drinks," Char interjected.

"That's horrible," Sawyer said.

"Plus, Tyne recognized him from Monday night, which corroborated Colby's claim." Sawyer put his arms around his mother.

"Mom, I should have been here. I know you were looking to make a major life change, but I don't think this is what you signed up for. Do you want to sell the inn and walk away? Maybe go back to teaching?" Max understood why her son might think that, but nothing was further from the truth. Max had found her purpose in this new endeavor. She didn't want to walk away.

"No way. I love this place, Sawyer. Pearla and I have it all under control. We've got grand plans. There's no way I'd leave. I regret anyone got hurt, and I wish I could have prevented it. This was no one's fault except Parker's."

Krista sighed. "That's not true. I feel awful and I'm so sorry. This was my fault. If I hadn't invited Parker here, none of this would have happened. I'm swearing off men."

"Now that would be a shame," Sawyer said.

Is he flirting?

"Parker wasn't who he said he was from the start. Of course, I wouldn't know that because I'm so naive." Krista put her head in her hands. Max thought she looked positively miserable.

"Give yourself a break. We can't all go around suspecting everyone of being out to get us. That's no way to live," Pearla comforted. "I've had my share. Some men are skilled at fooling people. They know just what to say, and it's everything we want to hear."

"I suppose. But I'm not keen to date again anytime soon. I should've seen the red flags. Like why did I always pay if he was so well-off? Why could I never see his house or meet his roommates or his parents? You get the picture." Everyone nodded sympathetically.

"Char, when you contacted me to meet you here, Parker was all interested in coming along. Now I know he must have researched you and found out you're wealthy and that I'm your only living relative." Krista began to sob, swiping her hand across her eyes to wipe her tears.

"Clearly, he figured if you were dead, I'd be rich and if he married me, so would he. It's sickening. I'm so embarrassed. I hope you know I only want your friendship, all of you. I hope you'll forgive me for what happened."

"There is nothing to forgive. None of this is your fault," Char reassured.

"I feel responsible. I should have known. Poor Rose McMartin. All she wanted was a romantic week with her husband. Instead, she gets a blow to the head and finds out her husband and so-called friend are having an affair."

"Oh, so Parker thought Rose was you, Aunt Char?" Sawyer asked.

"And he tried to kill her and make it look like an accident," Krista said. "We didn't even know he was in town. He kept texting me saying he'd be late. I bought it, of course."

"You really can't make this stuff up," Pearla added.

"He probably planned to knock me off too after we got married," Krista said disgustedly.

"What did Beth's murder have to do with this, though? How is that connected?" Sawyer asked.

This sounds like a bad soap opera script when you lay it all out.

"Sheriff Silva says Beth saw Parker on Monday, she was suspicious and she'd be able to identify him. So he got rid of the camera footage from the store and her too. He wasn't supposed to be in town. He screwed up his own alibi, so he had to get rid of her," Pearla explained.

"So complicated, and all for money," Sawyer stated, shaking his head.

"Sawyer, it usually is. Trust me. I read a lot of true crime. Money is a powerful motivator," Pearla explained.

"Oh, I almost forgot," Char said. "I have gifts. Be right back." The others waited as Char retrieved the packages from her room. Max received a scented candle.

"I love that it's Coastal Fog," she exclaimed. "Very appropriate." For Pearla, there were bath bombs.

"Char, you know me well," she said. And for Krista, the pendant necklace and matching earrings.

"I believe these will complete the set."

* * *

Ms. Singer was the last to check out. She lugged her heavy suitcase up to the front desk and set her key on the counter. It was hard to guess how she felt by her neutral expression, and Max assumed it would be the last time she'd see the famous, reclusive author.

"I hope you've enjoyed your stay, Ms. Singer. And I hope we'll see you again sometime." The author broke into a huge grin and slapped her hands on the counter.

"This is the most productive I've been in ages. I could not have asked for a better time. I even had a brief fling. Best it's over, since he accused me of murder." She winked at Max and laughed.

"Well, I'm thrilled to hear that, the part about it being productive as far as your writing goes. The fling too, I guess." *Shut up, Max. Stop talking!* "We would absolutely love to have you as our guest again here at Snowy Plover Inn."

"Bet on it," she said and left out the front doors with a flourish.

At ten that night, Max and Pearla sat up in the tower overlooking the inn's property. All the rooms were occupied.

Sawyer was comfortable in his loft bedroom and Char had turned in early wanting to get on the road in the morning. Krista had left midmorning with a tearful goodbye and hugs all around. Max looked forward to having her stay again. The three new employees had all shown up on time, and training was going well. They would make wonderful additions to the staff. Larry and Colby would stay employed as groundskeepers, having proved their loyalty beyond a doubt.

"This first week is one for the books," Max said with a satisfied sigh.

"I wouldn't change it for the world," Pearla said.

What's next?

Tee Time Tragedy at the Snowy Plover Inn

Come back and settle in at the quaint Snowy Plover Inn, where life is peaceful and relaxing—until it isn't.

It's been six months since the re-opening of the Snowy Plover Inn, the first week's drama all but forgotten. Spurred on by the construction of a first-class wellness center, just ten miles inland, the revitalization of sleepy Silvermist Point is underway. While some townies, including Maxine and Pearla, are excited to make it a destination, other residents wish to keep it a hidden gem.

Wealthy investors interested in purchasing and restoring the golf course, are staying at the inn. One is killed instantly when he takes an errant golf ball to the skull. Whoever did it, had perfect aim and the intent to kill.

When the Snowy Plover Inn is dubbed the 'Hotel of Death' in *The Silvermist Point of View*, Max and Pearla are compelled to get involved in solving the crime. They don't get far before their prime suspect, also staying at the inn, turns up dead. Not the best look for the town or the inn.

* * *

Books in the Snowy Plover Inn series:
Checked Out at the Snowy Plover Inn
Christmas at the Snowy Plover Inn (a holiday novella)

Thank you for taking the time to read *Checked Out at the Snowy Plover Inn*. If you enjoyed it please tell your friends, and I would be so grateful if you would consider posting a review. Word of mouth is an author's best friend, and very much appreciated.

Thank you,

Deanna Nese

Let's connect!
Facebook Deanna Nese: Author
Substack. @deannanese1
Instagram @deannaneseauthor
Twitter @deanna_nese
Pinterest: neseteach